Lassit
to Rescue
and Keep
from Reaching ... ...den Dragon!

"I much prefer shooting a rifle," Lanna Mitchell said, holding up the Colt. "I know I can't hit anything with this."

"If we had a rifle, I'd give it to you," Lassiter said. "Just stay low over your horse and go straight for them. We just need to surprise them."

Lasssiter positioned them for the charge as Lee and Wong Lin's men rode up. He waited until they reached just the right place along the trail, where the falling sun would blind them against the attack.

Lassiter yelled and spurred his horse into a dead run, with Lanna and Harold Mitchell coming out from the brush at the same time. Lassiter rode hard toward the leader, Wong Lin, and fired. But Wong Lin suddenly reined in his horse, and the man just next to him rode into the bullet.

Lassiter continued to ride straight at Wong Lin, who shouted oaths at him in Chinese. With only one good hand, Wong Lin was unable to shoot. Two of Wong Lin's men spurred their horses toward Lassiter, but were falling from their saddles before they could get off a shot.

Wong Lin was concentrating on Lassiter and did not see Lanna riding toward him. A flame burst from the barrel of her Colt . . .

Books by Loren Zane Grey

Published by POCKET BOOKS

LOREN ZANE GREY

LASSITER AND THE GOLDEN DRAGON

POCKET BOOKS

New York   London   Toronto   Sydney   Tokyo

An *Original* Publication of POCKET BOOKS

POCKET BOOKS, a division of Simon & Schuster Inc.
1230 Avenue of the Americas, New York, NY 10020

ISBN: 0-671-63896-3

First Pocket Books printing November 1989

10 9 8 7 6 5 4 3 2 1

POCKET and colophon are trademarks of Simon & Schuster Inc.

Printed in the U.S.A.

LASSITER AND THE GOLDEN DRAGON

1

THE SPRING THUNDERSTORM had just stopped and the streets of downtown San Francisco glistened with moisture. But the weather had done little to dampen the spirits of the bustling seaport town, and trolley cars carried citizens and sightseers from all over the world through what was now one of the fastest-growing cities in the entire country.

Nearly thirty years had passed since a cluster of tents had emerged along the harbor. A lot had happened, and as Lassiter rode into town from the north he saw how much it had changed, even in the four years since he had last come to the city by the bay.

The edge of the city along the docks still reminded him of the old days. Ships of every make and description were being unloaded or awaited their turn, anchored out in the water. The ships were filled with passengers, most of them seeing the new land for the first time.

Immigrants from the Far East were common. In fact, there were more Chinese here than any other group of immigrants. The Chinese mixed with miners and various frontiersmen who were either in town to spend what money they had, or were drifting through to catch gossip about jobs at developing frontier towns, or possibly some easy money staking a claim at a mother lode of gold somewhere out in the mountains.

It all looked the same to Lassiter, who had seen a number of boom towns spring up throughout the West. But San Francisco had been among the first of the settlements to come into being and grow into a large city almost overnight. And from this point were spreading out a lot of smaller settlements all along the main frontier trails and railways.

Lassiter had been riding nearly three days straight and the sight of the city refreshed him. Sundown was just a moment away as he eased his black stallion through the congestion, working past other riders on horseback, as well as carriages, wagons, and pedestrians. His destination was the finer, main section of the city. He was, in fact, headed for the luxurious and already infamous Palace Hotel.

It had been some time since Lassiter had last seen San Francisco, and he had come to relax. It felt good to see the city again—this time as an honored guest. He had traveled over a lot of the West and had decided the fall before to establish a permanent post office box in Denver. He had written a lot of friends and had answered a lot of the cards and letters that had been building up in his saddlebags.

After a cold winter of guarding a freight line through Colorado from road agents and hostile Indians, he had been excited to receive an invitation to the gala fundraising festival in San Francisco at the end of April.

It wasn't often that he was given the opportunity to be treated so well, by anybody. But this stroke of good fortune was attributable to the impression he had made on a wealthy man and his daughter a few years before.

It had been something he had just ridden into and had greatly benefited from in the end.

"We'll never forget you, Lassiter," is what Lanna Mitchell had told him. "And you're welcome to come back and work for me any time, just any time at all," Harold Mitchell had added. "You've done more for us than you can ever imagine."

In Lassiter's mind, it seemed his adventures a long ways to the north in the small boom town of Glitter Creek, Idaho Territory, had taken place just yesterday. Though not all of the events had been pleasant ones—indeed some had nearly cost him his life—he could still not forget the fine treatment given him by Harold Mitchell, nor the wondrous affections of Mitchell's beautiful daughter Lanna. Her warm and gracious face framed in long, red hair was a vision he often conjured in his mind on long, cold nights.

In the gold town of Glitter Creek, Lassiter had saved Harold Mitchell's daughter from abduction by road agents—not to mention his saving the town itself from control by the same thieves. Now Lanna Mitchell and her father were in San Francisco on business, as Mitchell was hoping to expand his interests from Glitter Creek into the mining territory along the railroads that were extending across the desert country of Nevada Territory.

Lassiter had gained the information from a letter attached to the invitation and knew no more of Mitchell's business plans than this, other than the fact that he realized Mitchell must be getting into something big.

The invitation had been co-signed by one of San Francisco's big politicians, a man named L. T. Farnham. It appeared as if Mitchell was backing Farnham's run for the city council, and the fund-raiser was to announce their partnership in developing some town in the heart of a desert deep in Nevada Territory.

Business and politics and that sort of thing had little

effect on Lassiter. He could take it or leave it. But with the comforting thoughts of a few days with plenty to eat and a good bed—as well as the chance to see Lanna Mitchell again—rolling through his head, Lassiter was eager to reach the main part of town and the Palace Hotel.

But first he would have to cross a segment of the city that he knew would be dangerous. To many people, this part of town had proved lethal.

He rode into the section known as Chinatown, where the population of Chinese immigrants had established their own cultural and political sanctuary in a country that was often hostile to them. It was their domain and no one who wasn't wanted there ever lasted long, especially after the sun went down.

It was easy to see how the Chinese had come to form their own fortress. Regarded by the other races as essentially inferior, the Chinese were pressed on all sides and made to feel unwelcome. No one else cared whether they remained or left again for their homeland.

As far as the Chinese were concerned, they wanted it that way. They had come across the Pacific merely in the hopes of making a quick fortune, so that they might return to their provinces and build a better future for their destitute families. Assimilating into the new culture in a new land of broken promises was something they neither expected nor cared to accomplish.

As Lassiter rode through the middle of Chinatown, he drew any number of glances. He made his way along Dupont Street, known locally as the Dupont Gai, where the population of Chinese was steadily increasing. Lassiter was noting how this part of town looked even rougher than during his last visit, when he thought the place couldn't look much worse.

There were any number of vagrants of all nationalities sprawled in various places at the edge of the streets and in the alleys. The majority of them were sick from opium, Lassiter knew, the drug of choice in the Orient. Its use was obviously getting more prevalent here in the land of promise, and the suffering was going to become worse before it got better.

"Hopheads" is what the addicts were called, at least when Lassiter had been here before. And he didn't think the name had changed any. All that had changed was the number of them lying wasted and useless, many near death. Chinatown had certainly gotten a lot bigger, and a lot uglier.

As Lassiter rode through the squalor, he knew he had little to fear. No matter how rough the area appeared, there was no one here who was going to challenge him for anything.

Clad as always in his black leather vest and pants, he both melded into the form of his black stallion and at the same time stood apart from the animal. What the onlookers noticed most was the two big black-handled Colt .44s, which stuck out prominently from his hips. Soon, many people were running from the street ahead of him.

Lassiter did not understand the reason for their fear of him. He was used to people watching him with a wary eye, but usually the reaction was not so desperate. These people couldn't move fast enough to get away.

He decided finally that the reason could lie in the possibility that this section of town was in some way under siege. For some reason, they might think he had appeared in town under hire to someone and could represent death to many of them.

As he rode further, Lassiter could see that the section of the street he was about to ride into was completely devoid of citizens. They had all moved out far ahead of his arrival. Lassiter immediately suspected something.

In the twilight, he could see only clusters of buildings with Oriental fronts along both sides of the street, lit by red lights. Otherwise there was nothing to see. But he could feel something, as if someone were watching him.

Lassiter brought his stallion to a stop and pulled one of his pistols. In but a few short moments, four men dressed in black Oriental clothing emerged from the shadows of an alley. Lassiter cocked his pistol. They all appeared to be holding pistols of their own at their sides, though none of them raised a weapon to fire.

They were obviously linked together in some sort of gang. Lassiter watched closely as they walked slowly, moving sideways across the street ahead of him.

One of them—who was the largest by far, and appeared to be the leader—moved ahead of the other three. Though he was dressed in Oriental fashion like the others and his hair was worn in a queue down his back, he looked far more Caucasion than Chinese.

Lassiter heard the big man speaking to the others in Chinese, then saying "gunfighter" to them in English. This made Lassiter think that they believed he had been sent by someone to enter their section of Chinatown, and that they meant to defend their territory.

Lassiter turned around and saw three more men dressed in the same style of black clothing taking position in the street behind him. They, too, held pistols at their sides. They held their ground a ways off.

Lassiter loosened the reins in his left hand and pulled his other Colt. Now both pistols were cocked. If he needed to start shooting, he could put three or four of the men in front of him down before they could react.

Lassiter then held his stallion still and waited to see what might develop. The four in front of him stood in the street started mumbling among themselves. They were obviously impressed by Lassiter's courage and cool manner. A man who was not easily frightened was a dangerous one when cornered.

Finally, Lassiter decided he would give the big leader an opportunity to state their reasons for detaining him before he shot his way past them.

"I know you speak English," Lassiter said to the big man, "and I want to know why you're blocking my path. I'll give you until the count of three to explain. If you don't, get ready to die."

"You don't shoot at us," the big one said quickly. "We just want to know your business here."

Listening to him speak, Lassiter realized his English was almost perfect. If this man of mostly Caucasian blood was an immigrant, he was not a recent one.

"Why didn't you just ask in the first place?" Lassiter wanted to know. "I'm just passing through here."

"Just passing through? To where?" The big man now seemed more confident.

"I said I'm just passing through," Lassiter admonished him. "To where is none of your business. Now, you let me through or I'll make my own way. Which will it be?"

"There's seven of us," the big man challenged. "You'll die."

Lassiter could tell by the way they were holding their weapons that they weren't good at gunfighting from a distance. And they didn't want to get any closer—not just yet.

"You'll die first, though," Lassiter promised him. "Then it won't make any difference to you who goes next. You won't be around to care."

The big man studied Lassiter. He didn't want to die and he knew Lassiter would make good on his promise. Lassiter decided not to give him any more time to figure out a plan to get to him, or give the others behind him the signal to open fire.

Lassiter kicked his stallion into a dead run. The big man yelled as Lassiter aimed his Colt at him. Lassiter didn't fire, as all four men in front of him then scattered like squawking chickens into the shadows of the alleys. Two of them even dropped their pistols in fright.

Once he was well past them and out of Chinatown, Lassiter slowed his horse. He felt lucky they weren't aggressive enough to have started a shootout. And even though they weren't well versed in gunfighting, he might have run into others who could shoot.

But it was over now, and he gave it no more thought as he entered the finer section of the city. The streets were lit up with gaslights as he made his way along Market Street toward the most striking new building San Francisco had to offer. He was beginning once again to get the feeling that he had brought to the city with him—the feeling that he was soon going to be having the time of his life.

2

WITH THOUGHTS OF A FESTIVE TIME running wildly through his head, Lassiter continued up Market Street, to where it met at a three-way corner with Geary and Kearny streets. He rode past Lotta's Fountain, where people were gathered to see out the last part of the evening before going home.

The Palace Hotel stood out as a seven-story monster of brick, erected around carved hardwood and marble. It was *the* landmark of the city, with a huge American flag flying from a pole atop the last story facing Market Street. As Lassiter had learned in the letter from Harold Mitchell, the hotel had opened less than six months before and was booked solid nightly.

Lassiter rode his black stallion past carriages filled with dignitaries. They all looked at Lassiter questioningly and began to talk. But when Lassiter dismounted and presented the invitation to a porter, his horse was taken immediately to the stable connected with the hotel.

Lassiter passed into the lobby, which was filled with more dignitaries, laughing and conversing. In his customary black leathers, with his twin Colt pistols at his side, Lassiter made his usual startling impression, and everyone turned to stare momentarily. But most of them were busy with their conversations and immediately went back to their topics.

If Lassiter excited some curiosity among the guests, so then did the guests seem curious to Lassiter. But still more interesting to him were the furnishings. Standing on the inner court, Lassiter marveled at the expanse of marble, rosewood, and ebony, lit from top to bottom by rows of gaslights. The light reflected off tiers of balconies, supported by long columns and arches, and off of five hydraulic "rising rooms," which carried guests and patrons to the uppermost levels.

Lassiter checked in at the desk and was given the key to one of the best suites in the house. An assistant manager assured him that Harold Mitchell had made sure his horse was cared for in the best manner possible.

At no time in recent memory could Lassiter remember having been given this kind of treatment. He wondered if the event might not last a week or so. He could get used to this.

The assistant manager then directed Lassiter toward the Grand Dining Room, where everyone was beginning to congregate. "I have been instructed to advise you that your presence is desired as soon as you arrive," the assistant manager said. "Mr. Harold Mitchell and his party are expecting you."

Lassiter thanked the assistant manager and made his way among the dozens of busboys and waiters who moved through the guests with trays of drinks. Along one wall an orchestra was getting itself seated on a stage. It appeared to be a large and extravagant celebration, larger than he had imagined.

Lassiter was hailed with a shout from nearby. Approaching him was Harold Mitchell, holding a glass of whiskey and smoking a big cigar. He was followed by his daughter, Lanna, and a contingent of dignitaries. They were all curious about him, but it was obvious to Lassiter that the dignitaries much preferred the vision of Lanna to his own.

She stood out from the entire group, as striking as ever. She wore a black satin dress trimmed in gold and white, with gloves to match. Her long red hair streamed in ringlets out from under a dainty black cap fringed with miniature dangling balls of silk.

Harold Mitchell greeted Lassiter with a rousing handshake and a clap on the back. Lanna smiled and extended her hand gracefully. Lassiter bent forward and kissed the back of her glove, much to the surprise of those watching. Lanna was not surprised, however, as she knew that Lassiter might do just about anything that came to mind.

"It's good to see you again, Lanna," Lassiter said in greeting.

Lanna's smile widened. "The pleasure is equally mine, I'm sure," she said. "If you'll excuse me, I'll join some of the ladies now. I'm certain you and Father have a great deal to discuss."

Lassiter nodded, and Lanna eased her way past him to where a group of women were seated around a table, drinking wine brought by waiters and discussing the events of the evening. Then he turned to Harold Mitchell, who was smiling.

"My daughter thinks a great deal of you, Lassiter," he commented. "She has been looking forward to this trip."

"I'll have to say that those long miles on horseback to get here were eased considerably by the thought of conversation with her," Lassiter admitted.

"Well, I sure am glad you could make it, Lassiter," Mitchell said, beaming. "How've you been?"

Lassiter nodded slightly. "Each day's been a new one, so far. I take them one at a time."

Mitchell chuckled. "For a man in your profession, that's the only way you can do it."

"For a man in *any* profession," Lassiter corrected him. "But mine in particular."

"Yes, I'd have to agree," Mitchell said with a laugh, chomping on the cigar. He pulled one from his pocket and handed it to Lassiter. The aroma of bourbon in the cigar was strong as Lassiter allowed Mitchell to light it for him.

"You're doing things up right here, I'd say," Lassiter commented to Mitchell.

"It's a special night," Mitchell said with a nod. He pointed across the court to a man who stood out in the crowd, conversing with a number of guests. Lassiter noticed the man was flanked by two bodyguards, both packing big Colts under their black dinner jackets.

"Is that the man this celebration is in honor of?" Lassiter asked.

Mitchell nodded. "L. T. Farnham. There's a lot going on in this city and he's right in the middle of it. He's somebody I'd like you to meet right away."

Lassiter followed Mitchell across the floor to where the group surrounded L. T. Farnham. The crowd parted and allowed them into the inner circle. Lassiter noticed that Farnham's two hard-looking bodyguards were not softened in the least by the expensive suits they wore.

Lassiter stood next to Mitchell, while Farnham's two bodyguards eyed him sternly, trying to measure what he was all about. Farnham was dressed more expensively than anyone else except Harold Mitchell. He was a little taller than Mitchell, much thinner, and certainly much more contained in his mannerisms. He was slick and used to seeing what he could get out of people from the first time he met them. Lassiter could sense that this man was a user.

But tonight Farnham wanted to appear his casual best. He wanted everyone impressed with his importance, and though he, too, was smoking a cigar, he did not have it in his mouth much but instead rolled it nervously between his thumb and forefinger.

Harold Mitchell introduced him to Lassiter. "This is L. T. Farnham, who's soon going to be a distinguished member of the city council—and, I might add, soon to be also a business partner of mine."

Lassiter nodded and took Farnham's hand. Farnham's grip was decidedly lax.

"You appear to be a man of the trails and badlands, Mr. Lassiter," Farnham said with a slightly crooked smile, blowing cigar smoke. "Aren't you a bit out of your element here in San Francisco?"

"Only a fool judges a man by his 'element,'" Lassiter pointed out, calmly dragging on his cigar. "Blindness is indeed a sore affliction."

Farnham blushed and grunted faintly. "I suppose that's true. Well, I'd better get ready to give my speech." He looked at his two bodyguards, then nodded to Harold Mitchell as he turned and walked away. He was followed by most of the people who had gathered around, and many of them stared at Lassiter as they made their way to the tables that were now being set by waiters.

"Your new business partner, eh?" Lassiter said to Mitchell when they were gone. "How did you come across him?"

"I've been looking for a new venture to invest in," Mitchell told Lassiter. "Similar to what I did up in Glitter Creek, a venture whose success, I might add, is due in a large part to your having been there during the hard times at the beginning."

Lassiter nodded and puffed again on the cigar. His time working for Mitchell in Glitter Creek had indeed been an adventure of an unusual kind, and Mitchell was still grateful to him for having saved the town from the road agents.

"In any event," Mitchell continued, "I spread the

word among my friends here in San Francisco that I needed some ideas and some backing. There are any number of people here familiar with what I've done up in Idaho Territory. So the word got around and I heard from L. T. Farnham almost immediately.''

"In my opinion, you should have ignored his correspondence," Lassiter said dryly.

"You never were one for hiding your opinions, were you, Lassiter?" Harold Mitchell said with a good-natured laugh. "I suppose he does seem a little stuffy to someone who doesn't know him all that well."

"How well do you know him, Harold?" Lassiter asked, inhaling on the cigar once again.

"I'm not much more than well acquainted, I'll have to admit," Mitchell said. "I've only met and talked with him in the last couple of days. But he comes highly recommended by some close friends. And, as you can see, he's headed for high places politically."

Lanna then came over from where she had been talking with the group of women. "Father, I believe they're waiting for you to join them," she said, tilting her head toward the crowd of men getting themselves seated at the head table for Farnham's speech.

"Yes, I suppose so," Harold Mitchell said with a nod. "We should all go over, shouldn't we?"

"Please, Father," Lanna insisted, "I'm not feeling all that well and I don't think I could take a lot of being seating in here."

"Well, I'm sorry," Mitchell told his daughter. "Why don't you keep Lassiter company while he eats some dinner. I'll join you when this thing is over with."

Lanna smiled. "That is an excellent idea, Father. You have a good time with your friends."

Harold Mitchell kissed his daughter on the cheek and turned for the head table. Lassiter extended his arm and Lanna allowed him to escort her out of the large room and across the lobby to a small and more private section for dining. Lassiter could see that the waiters knew Lanna very well already and were there immediately to seat them and serve them. She ordered a small glass of brandy, while Lassiter ordered a bottle of wine to go with his meal.

"Not many grapes on the other side of the mountains," he commented. "And most saloon keepers won't have wine with their other liquors. I'd best take advantage while I can."

Lanna laughed. "You haven't changed at all, have you. Always mixing refinement with your hard nature."

"Hard nature?" Lassiter raised his eyebrows.

Lanna laughed. "Just sometimes." Then her mood turned more somber. "I wish Father wasn't mixed up with that Farnham character."

Lassiter put his cigar out and poured himself a glass of wine. "I thought he wasn't tied up with him—yet."

"Well, not yet, not officially," Lanna said. "But that's only a matter of a few hours away."

"What's going to take place?" Lassiter asked.

"Father has had it in his mind for some time to expand," Lanna began. "He advertised here in San Francisco and Farnham gave him this—to my way of thinking, crazy—notion of building up some town in the Nevada desert, well east of here. I don't understand it, and I don't understand why Father seems to be going for the idea. I think he's just mesmerized by Farnham and his political ambitions."

"But your father isn't a fool in business affairs," Lassiter pointed out. He poured Lanna more brandy and himself more wine. "What makes you unsure of the idea?"

"I'll have to admit that he's done very well in Glitter Creek, thanks to you," Lanna replied with a nod. "But Farnham has convinced Father he should go in and build up the community like he did at Glitter Creek. This little place is called Creosote Pass, or some dreadful thing like that. What is 'creosote' anyway?''

"Creosote is a desert shrub," Lassiter told her. "They use the sticky black liquid from the plant as a preservative in railroad ties.''

"All the more reason not to go there," Lanna said, sipping her brandy and raising her eyebrows. "What if you step on one of those bushes?''

"You have to squeeze pretty hard to get much out," Lassiter said. "Besides, you don't weigh enough to have to worry.''

Lanna laughed again, despite her concern.

"So, how does Farnham fit into all this?" Lassiter continued.

"It was Farnham who told him about the town. He wants to go into partnership with my father. He'll put up the majority of the money, or so he says, if Father will go into the town and oversee the initial construction of a bank and hotel.''

Lassiter watched the waiter bring his meal. He thought for a moment while he tested the steaming duck in front of him with his fork.

"Why would Farnham have any interest in a little rathole desert town?" Lassiter wondered aloud. "He's a big man here in San Francisco. There can't be that much money out there.''

"There's gold on both sides of the area," Lanna said. "I guess people are getting rich quick. But that's not what's attracting Farnham and Father. They seem to think Creosote Pass could become a major stopover area.''

"Are you saying the railroad is going through there eventually?" Lassiter asked.

"Father thinks he knows something about a spur line being built there, or something," Lanna explained. "If the railroad does build through there, Creosote Pass will be the only stop all across that desert country. Father is probably right in thinking that that little town will boom.''

''I guess it pays to know what's going to be built and where,'' Lassiter said, raising a forkful of roast duck toward his mouth. ''But I wouldn't care if the stakes were set for big winnings. I wouldn't have anything to do with Farnham if I was your father.''

''Should I try to talk him out of the venture?'' Lanna asked.

Lassiter swallowed. ''I would certainly try to talk him out of it. I'm going to tell him that myself. I've already expressed my feelings to him once, but I want him to hear them again.''

''What if he doesn't listen?'' Lanna asked.

''There's no way to stop him if he insists on going into business with Farnham,'' Lassiter said. ''I just hope he doesn't have to learn something about Farnham he doesn't want to know. Something that he might have to learn the hard way.''

3

LASSITER RAISED HIS FORK for another bite of duck, but stopped when he saw two Oriental men, both large and dressed in red uniforms, hurrying across the room. They reminded him immediately of the men dressed in black that he had encountered in Chinatown.

Lassiter continued to watch the two as they barged past patrons and waiters, knocking over tables and chairs on their way toward the back entrance. The disruption in the room was immediate and many people ran the other way.

The two Orientals were soon followed by L. T. Farnham's two bodyguards, both with their guns drawn. The bodyguards rushed along the path left by the two Orientals, knocking down more tables and people, before finally exiting out the back themselves.

No one settled down immediately. Everyone was talking and some were leaving their meals, just to get out. It was going to take some time before the room quieted. The manager and most of his help were out working to calm everyone.

"What do you suppose that was all about?" Lanna asked Lassiter.

"I don't know," Lassiter answered. "The only thing I can think of is that those two Orientals must have been after Farnham for some reason. But Farnham's men seemed to have those two on the run, so maybe they stopped them before they got to him."

"Why would they be after Farnham?" Lanna asked. "Is there somebody who doesn't want him elected for some reason?"

"That could be possible," Lassiter agreed. "I wouldn't be surprised if Farnham doesn't have a lot of enemies. That's why he keeps those two men with him all the time."

Before Lassiter could get back to his meal, both he and Lanna were startled by a sudden outburst of screaming and yelling that was coming from somewhere on the main floor of the hotel. Lassiter and Lanna both realized that something was happening in the Grand Dining Room. The sound of gunshots punctured the air. Lassiter was immediately to his feet.

"You'd better stay here," he advised Lanna. "There's shooting."

"I will not stay here!" Lanna told him flatly. "I won't wait behind and wonder if Father is in some kind of trouble."

Lassiter knew he wasn't going to be able to keep Lanna back in safety; she was too shook up already and anxious about her father. He would have to watch her as best he could.

"Stay behind me and don't get out in the open," Lassiter advised her. "Stay close to the walls and don't expose yourself. Do you understand?"

"I understand," Lanna said. "Let's go."

Lassiter realized there was now a lot of trouble going on in the Grand Dining Room. He knew now that the two Orientals had been tied into the whole thing, possibly to draw Farnham's two bodyguards away from him. Now Farnham was definitely vulnerable, and Lanna's father as well.

Lassiter hurried out of the dining room, with Lanna right behind him. They pushed past groups of startled people who were milling in all directions, stepping over the bodies of hotel security men who had been killed.

In the ballroom, the entire congregation was a mass of confusion. People were running everywhere from a group of Chinese men who had entered the ballroom and were bent on a set pattern of extermination.

These men were all dressed in red, just like the two who had run through the dining room. Though they were Chinese, most of them were large in stature and carried what appeared to be battle-axes or large hatchets. Lassiter watched one of them bring his ax down upon the head of a man who had fallen at his feet.

Others among the attackers brought out pistols and began to shoot at various individuals in the room. Lassiter was certain the killers were not choosing their victims at random, but instead were selecting them as if they had been seeking them out specifically at this function.

The men who were being killed were dignitaries and politicians—people of high stature in the city. There was a reason for it and the first thought that came to Lassiter's mind was that somebody wanted all the people in the city who supported L. T. Farnham fitted into pine boxes.

Lassiter quickly found Harold Mitchell and united him with Lanna, then got them out of the dining room. He knew that Harold Mitchell would likely be on the list and that L. T. Farnham certainly had to be a major target.

Lassiter gave Lanna and Harold Mitchell explicit instructions to stay under cover and returned, where he found himself standing between Farnham and two of the killers.

Farnham had retreated toward one of the doors but was now jammed against other people who were trying to get out. The two killers were approaching and seemed startled at seeing Lassiter with both Colts drawn. After getting rid of the hotel security people, they had not expected to encounter anyone else with firearms who really knew how to use them.

But seeing Lassiter did not stop their charge and Lassiter thumbed the hammers on both pistols, killing them both easily.

Upon hearing the shots, others of the faction turned their attention on Lassiter. One of them, a huge Oriental man with a large hatchet, charged in front of two others. Lassiter fired into him three times before he stumbled to his knees. He refused to go down, but fought to keep himself on his knees, coughing blood out onto his massive chest and stomach.

Lassiter had no time to finish him, as the other two began shooting. Their aim was reckless, but they would soon be close enough that they would make some of their shots count.

Lassiter fired both pistols again, sending the two sprawling over the bodies of the dignitaries they had killed moments before. The huge man with the hatchet tried to rise, his eyes narrowed in pain and hatred. Farnham's two bodyguards burst into the room and filled him with bullets.

The other Chinese killers then turned and began a hasty but orderly retreat. Lassiter reloaded quickly, but chanced no more shots. There had been enough people killed as it was and the way the others were running wildly around the room, any stray shot could hit one of them.

The killers were moving along the edge of the crowd of terrified guests, their eyes on Lassiter. One of them—who appeared to be the leader—held up at the door and raised his axe in the air, swearing an oath at him. It was obvious to Lassiter that whoever they were, they did not intend to forget him. They would no doubt be looking for revenge.

The pandemonium in the room did not settle down at all after the killers' retreat. There was considerable crying and grieving over the men who had been killed and some concern over whether or not the killers would return.

Someone had already gone for the town marshal. There were men coming in with guns drawn who had been called in from the streets, as well as a number of doctors. Lassiter turned to see Farnham's two bodyguards standing near the politician, who looked at Lassiter a moment before turning away to talk with guests who were concerned about his well-being.

Lassiter hadn't expected a thank-you from Farnham. But he didn't expect the glare he got from one of the bodyguards—a fine piece of gratitude for saving someone's life.

Shrugging it off, Lassiter went to the huge Chinese killer's body and turned him over. He noted a tattoo on his right forearm, a series of Chinese symbols on either side of a small dragon. Lassiter saw right away that this had to be the mark of some specific gang who had come with the intended purpose of getting rid of Farnham and his main supporters.

Lanna and her father appeared, and Lassiter walked over to where they stood near one wall, viewing the results of the attack. Lanna still showed the effects of shock, but was relieved that her father hadn't been in the middle of the mess.

"Maybe you should sit down for a little while," Lassiter suggested to her.

"I'm fine, thank you, Lassiter," Lanna insisted. "It's Father I'm worried about. I believe those men would have tried to kill him, had they found him in time. I want him to retire to his room, where he will be safe if they come back again."

"It's not likely they will be back again," Lassiter

assured her. "They didn't get the job done right the first time. They will have to wait for another opportunity. Tonight is no good for them any longer."

"It still makes me nervous," Lanna said.

"Just don't you worry any longer," Harold Mitchell told his daughter. "We won't stray very far from Lassiter, here, and there won't be any reason to be concerned."

"Do you have any idea what might have brought those killers in?" Lassiter asked him.

"I can't tell you, Lassiter," Mitchell answered honestly. "It seems obvious, though, that they had things planned thoroughly. If you hadn't been here, well, who knows what all might have happened. I have to thank you."

The city marshal and a number of deputies suddenly arrived and sealed off the area. No one was to come or go anywhere until they were finished questioning and gathering information.

"We might be in for a long evening," Mitchell told Lassiter. "I'm sorry about this. I guess you wouldn't have come if you had suspected you were riding into this instead of a relaxing few days with your boots off and your feet up."

"It couldn't be helped, so don't blame yourself," Lassiter told him. "Besides, I've never been able to spend any more than a few hours with my boots off before trouble hit. I guess this place isn't any different than any other."

The marshal began his questioning. Lassiter recognized him as Jess Markham. Jess had obviously come a long way since their first meeting in the middle of a shootout.

Lassiter had found Jess Markham, then a drifter, shooting his way out of a Texas border town. It was shortly after the South had surrendered to the North and Markham had trailed a gang of Comancheros into an adobe village called Del Rio. The Comancheros had caught him trying to steal his horse back.

Lassiter remembered how he had innocently rode in on the incident and had nearly gotten himself shot up. When the Comancheros had turned their fire on him as well, he had more than evened the odds for Markham by shooting five Comancheros from in front of a small saloon. Markham had told him he would be forever grateful.

And now they met again, under very similar circumstances. To Lassiter's way of thinking, it was odd to see Jess Markham here in San Francisco. Markham was tall and raw-boned, with a wind-whipped look to his features, someone you would expect to ride in out of a sandstorm and ask for dry mescal. But now he was dressed in a tailored black suit and top hat. He appeared to Lassiter to be a cowboy off the trail who'd somehow found himself jammed into a coat and tie.

But it looked as if Markham knew his job. And Lassiter noted as well, as he watched the marshal survey the carnage in the room, that Markham didn't seem too surprised at what had taken place. He was looking at the bodies and taking notes and ordering his men around like he'd done this before—maybe any number of times before.

"Do you know that marshal?" Harold Mitchell asked Lassiter.

"I know him quite well," Lassiter replied with a nod. "I think I'll spend some time with him and get to the bottom of all this."

"We'll wait for you," Lanna then told Lassiter. "I'm still worried about those killers. I think they'll come back. Could you get that marshal to leave some men here at the hotel for security?"

Though he didn't think the gang would return, not with men watching for them now, Lassiter could understand Lanna's concern.

"I'll do what I can," he promised.

While Lanna and her father moved away to talk with some of the other dignitaries, Lassiter turned his attention to learning about what had brought the killers into the hotel with the purpose of killing notable people. He knew Jess Markham would have some answers.

Markham had noticed Lassiter upon first entering the room. Still, a number of people continued to point Lassiter out to him and it wasn't long before the two of them came together and shook hands.

"I might have known it was you," Markham said, sporting a broad grin. "I heard a big gunman dressed in black wiped out half of a hatchet gang in here. Doesn't look like they were far from wrong."

"They killed a lot of people before I got here to fight them," Lassiter said. "They had it planned."

"You're right," Markham nodded. "They had it planned real good. But you spoiled it for them, and they won't forget you. You can bet a good horse on that."

Lassiter recalled the oath the large gang leader had yelled at him as they departed.

"You called them hatchet gangs?" he said to Markham.

"Tong gangs is what they call themselves," Markham explained. "But they're noted for killing their victims with hatchets. Not a pretty sight."

Lassiter nodded, watching medical people moving the dead and injured out. "Yeah, that's an understatement. But what brought them in here to begin with?"

"There's a whole story to this, a pretty long one," Markham replied. "What do you say I buy you a drink?"

4

LASSITER FOLLOWED MARKHAM into a quaint drinking parlor at the far end of a corridor leading out of the hotel. It was packed with men discussing the events of the evening. They moved and stared after Markham and Lassiter as the two men found a quiet corner at the end of the bar.

Lassiter downed a whiskey that Markham poured for him. Then he smiled and looked at Markham's suit.

"Appears to me that lawmen in big cities dress a lot like politicians. When you up for election?"

Markham coughed on his whiskey. Then he managed a grin himself. "You won't find me up spouting a lot of promises to nobody. Ever."

Lassiter continued to tease him. "You're dressed for the part."

"This ain't Del Rio, or some small trail stop somewhere," Markham pointed out, pouring another round. "I'm in charge of a lot of men and I have to fit a dress code. I don't mind; it pays the bills a lot better than most anything else you can find."

"I'd say you'd have to use your gun a lot around here," Lassiter suggested. "There's some mean boys come out after dark in these parts."

"I get the job done," Markham said. "You saved a bunch of those people from getting themselves hacked and shot up tonight. How do you happen to be in the city, anyway?"

"Harold Mitchell invited me," Lassiter told him. "He's one of the men who sponsored this bash here tonight."

Markham nodded. "I know the name. I heard he's fixing to get himself into business with L. T. Farnham."

Lassiter took note of Markham's tone, as if his advice would certainly be against something like that. He sipped his whiskey and studied Markham.

"Do you know something about Farnham that Harold Mitchell doesn't?"

"I don't know how well Mitchell knows Farnham," Markham replied. "But if he intends to go into business with Farnham, he'd best get on the good side of the Ming Chins, one of the biggest hatchet gangs in Chinatown."

"Tell me more about these hatchet gangs," Lassiter said. "I think I ran into one of them early tonight while crossing through Chinatown. They were dressed in black."

"That's the Ming Chins," Markham said, downing a swallow. "They're tied in with Farnham. Did they know who you were?"

"I don't think so," Lassiter replied. "They must have thought I was invading their territory."

"And you got by them without shooting?"

"I took my chances," Lassiter said. "I was lucky."

"There's a number of those strongarm gangs building up in Chinatown," Markham explained. "Back in China they're called the *boo how doy,* which is Chinese for 'Hatchet Sons.' They've been at each others' throats a long time over there and now they've brought it across the water. They've been getting stronger each year. Deal in drugs—opium mostly. They also shanghai women for pleasure houses. But they get to fighting among themselves over territories. You know, the same old thing."

"You're sure Farnham is tied in with one of those groups?" Lassiter asked.

"I'm sure, and tied in real deep," Markham said with a definite nod. "I don't have any doubt about it. Farnham's been bankrolling the Ming Chins. Has been for some time. He's getting a piece of a lot of pies now. The word is, he's expanding. He wants the territory now ruled by the Ta Kuos, who some call the Red Killers, the bunch that was here tonight."

"It would seem reasonable that they would want to stop him," Lassiter said. "But couldn't they do that on the street and not have to take the chance they did tonight? You don't just rush into a place like this and not worry about losing men."

"That's a good point," Markham agreed, "and they usually stick to the streets and alleys. And ordinarily they wouldn't think of coming into the Palace Hotel like they did tonight. But the Ta Kuos must have wanted Farnham dead real bad, and anyone else who's associated with him."

"Is Farnham helping the Ming Chins in their fight with the Ta Kuos?" Lassiter asked.

"It seems that he is," Markham replied. "In a big way. And he doesn't know what he's got himself into."

"So they'll be after him again," Lassiter commented. "And likely after Harold Mitchell as well."

"I would figure you to be right," Markham said. "Farnham did something that the Ta Kuos want revenge for bad. And they'll have it before they give up."

Markham went on to explain that Farnham had

taken it upon himself to try to put a quick end to the war by sending Ming Chin killers over to China to get rid of the main men among the Ta Kuos. They succeeded in killing two of the ringleaders before being found in an alley in small pieces.

"So you think Farnham was trying to get rid of the strongest of the Ta Kuos, so he could have his way here?" Lassiter asked.

"That would be my guess," Markham said with a nod. "Now the Ta Kuos know what the Ming Chins are up to and that's what caused this thing here tonight."

Lassiter nodded. "And the Ta Kuos were attempting to put a firm and quick stop to Farnham, and send a message to the Ming Chins, all in one night."

Markham nodded. "There's no doubt in my mind that they came to get rid of Farnham and his supporters, and probably Harold Mitchell, too. Good thing you were here. I hope you know Mitchell well enough to consider him that kind of friend."

"He is that kind of friend," Lassiter said, vouching for Mitchell's honesty. "He wouldn't have even considered getting mixed up with Farnham had he known about this."

Lassiter finished his whiskey and poured another, thinking of the mess Harold and Lanna Mitchell had gotten themselves into. But maybe they weren't entirely into the mess yet—they weren't if Mitchell hadn't formally entered into any agreements with Farnham.

"What are your plans now, Lassiter?" Markham asked.

"It looks to me now like I'll be having a short stay," Lassiter replied. "I'll tell Mitchell what you told me and he'll likely head on back up to Idaho, where he came from."

"I hope he leaves in a hurry," Markham said. "He doesn't want any part of this, and neither do you.

Chinatown will really be on edge now. Just so it doesn't spill over here any more than it has. They'll want you now, just as bad as they want anybody.''

"Are you worried about me?" Lassiter asked.

Markham grunted. "We haven't got enough coffins to keep up with what can happen when you get in the middle of a shootout. I can't do much in Chinatown any more, but I just want this part of town to be as peaceful as I can make it.''

Lassiter smiled. "Maybe I can clean up the hatchet gangs around here and save me a lot of future trouble. Do I get a fancy suit like yours?" Lassiter asked.

"I can order one," Markham said, his eyebrows raising. "If you want to be official, I'll make you first deputy."

Lassiter laughed. "You can handle it. I'm not much for the big city, not as a steady diet. But maybe just for tonight you could give me some authority and leave a few of your men here at the hotel, just in case.''

"I've thought about leaving some men," Markham said. "And I'll give you the authority to do things as you see fit. Just don't start a war of your own.''

Markham shook Lassiter's hand. "I've got to get back to work. If you need anything more before tomorrow, send for me. And if I don't see you again, take care of yourself.''

Lassiter watched Markham shoulder his way through the throng and out the door. He had gotten to know Markham pretty well after that day with the Comancheros down in Del Rio; they had ridden together for a while after that. He could tell that Markham was worried now—plenty worried—and that tonight was likely just the beginning of the trouble.

After one more whiskey, Lassiter made his way out of the drinking parlor and back into the Grand Dining Room. He saw that Mitchell was discussing business with some of those who still remained. Another, smaller, group was gathered around L. T. Farnham. Otherwise most of the crowd had left, concerned that trouble would return again and that they would not be as lucky as before.

Everything had changed now since the coming of the Ta Kuo hatchet men. There was a sense of urgency in the air. The dead and wounded had been carried out, but the floor still contained bloodstains that waiters were cleaning up—none of them Chinese, however. The Chinese waiters would rather lose their jobs than touch the blood of a hatchet man.

Lanna was again conversing with some of the wives and daughters of the guests still remaining. But now there was no laughing or light talk among them.

Lassiter noticed, as he crossed the floor to reach Harold Mitchell, how Farnham watched him from his group of men. There was little doubt in Lassiter's mind that Farnham was now very uneasy.

"I think we should talk for a little while," Lassiter said to Mitchell. "I wouldn't interrupt you, but I don't think it can wait."

Mitchell excused himself from the group and followed Lassiter to a corner of the room.

"You seem to have urgent news," Mitchell said.

"I've learned some things from the marshal that could save you a lot of trouble," Lassiter said. "L. T. Farnham might not be the best individual to put your trust in. It seems he's linked with one of the hatchet gangs from Chinatown—a group called the Ming Chins."

"Farnham? Involved with a gang? How could that be?" Mitchell was both startled and unbelieving. "Did you hear this from the marshal?"

Lassiter nodded. "He should know. He's responsible for keeping the peace here. To do that, he has to know a lot of things about what's going on and who's trying to grab power."

"How did the marshal say Farnham was involved?"

Mitchell asked, his eyebrows pressed down heavily.

Lassiter related how Farnham seemed to be bankrolling an ever-increasing opium trade, and how Farnham was now pushing to expand his operations—even to the point of sending killers overseas to China, in hopes of eliminating the competition's main power structure right away.

Mitchell took a deep breath. "I would hate to accuse a man of something like that unless it were true."

Lassiter had expected Mitchell to hold fast to his beliefs that Farnham was a sound man. Such had been the case in Glitter Creek when Lassiter had worked for him and had pointed out that the banker was tied in with a gang of road agents. Harold Mitchell seemed to have a knack for picking bad business partners.

Lassiter looked over to where Farnham was staring at him. "There is but one way to get this all sorted out," he suggested to Mitchell. "I think we'd best get him aside and talk to him. Ask him what he knows about all this. Right away."

Mitchell nodded. He was aware that he was going to have to know the truth before he could commit himself to a business venture with Farnham.

Lassiter walked beside Mitchell, and the two of them broke into Farnham's group. Farnham turned away. He didn't want to face Lassiter, for he knew this stranger dressed in black had any number of questions he would want answered. And it would be hard to lie to him. His two bodyguards just stared. Farnham finally tried to explain that he had no idea that the night would be disrupted in the way it had.

"I had no idea this was going to happen, either," Harold Mitchell spoke up. "But we need to discuss the matter. We can do it here and now, or adjourn to someplace more private." He waited for Farnham's response.

Farnham looked back and forth from Mitchell to

Lassiter. There was no way he was going to get out of it and he knew the only way he could save himself was to continue to act as surprised as the others. He couldn't afford to have Harold Mitchell discard his plans to have him as a business partner.

"Why don't we have the waiter bring us a bottle and take that table right over there," Farnham suggested. He led the way and told a waiter as he walked what he wanted brought in for them.

When they were seated, Lassiter got right to the point.

"I had a long discussion with Jess Markham," he began. "He tells me the Ta Kuos and the Ming Chins are beginning a war in Chinatown."

Farnham pleaded ignorance. "What do you mean? A gang war of some kind?"

"I thought you were running for commissioner?" Lassiter said. "Surely you must know about the hatchet gangs and the trouble they're causing."

Lassiter noticed Farnham's face flushing. The two bodyguards remained rigid. The waiter brought whiskey and Farnham poured everyone drinks.

"I try to stay away from that element," Farnham told Lassiter and Harold Mitchell. "I'm sure you can understand that. I have a reputation to uphold. So why don't we talk about Creosote Pass in Nevada Territory, and all the money to be had there."

"I've been thinking about that," Harold Mitchell told Farnham. "I'd like a little more time to decide whether or not a business partnership would really benefit me."

Now Farnham's face turned deep red. "What are you saying? You don't want to do the deal in Nevada with me now?"

"I just said I needed more time," Mitchell repeated.

"You don't need any more time," Farnham said forcefully, losing his self-control entirely. "The sooner we get this thing rolling, the sooner we can be making money."

"I said I'll have to think it over," Mitchell said decisively. "I can't see the reason for the rush. The railroad spur isn't scheduled to be built for another year yet. Isn't that what you told me?"

"Yes," Farnham nodded, "but we don't want somebody else beating us out there. You're a good developer and I've got lots of money. We've got to go right now."

"Not right now," Mitchell said flatly. "Not until I've made up my mind whether or not I even want to go out there. I may take a trip there to see the place first."

"You don't need to do that," Farnham argued. "It's just sand and brush. But when the railroad gets there, people will be needing accommodations."

Mitchell said nothing more, and there was a tense silence at the table. Finally, Farnham could stand it no longer.

"What's the matter, Mitchell?" he finally asked. "Are you worried about me or something? What's the matter here? Are you starting to listen to all the hearsay?"

"I was not aware of the hearsay," Mitchell said quickly. "What hearsay?"

Farnham shrugged. "I just thought you might have heard something you didn't like, that's all."

"What could that be?" Mitchell pressed.

"There is always something that's said by enemies that is designed to create havoc for a man seeking office," Farnham said, gulping his drink.

Lassiter watched Farnham squirm in his chair. He wasn't going to be able to dodge Harold Mitchell's questions. He was already exposing himself to a degree, and would likely soon incriminate himself completely.

Lassiter noted also that the two bodyguards were glaring at him. They were angry with him for putting Farnham against the wall. That was just the way Lassiter wanted it, and now he would just sit back and wait to see what kind of trouble they might want to start.

5

LASSITER AND MITCHELL both continued to listen intently while L. T. Farnham became more and more defensive. He was beginning to show that the pressure was really bothering him now.

"We've become good friends, Harold," Farnham told Mitchell. "I don't understand all the questions."

"If we're going into business, I want to know what to expect from my partner," Mitchell said. "You can understand that."

"Certainly," Farnham agreed. "But there's nothing to worry about."

"You still haven't told us what that hearsay is you talked about before," Lassiter said.

"It doesn't matter," Farnham said.

"It does matter," Lassiter said. "I can tell you what I heard. Or do you want to tell us yourself?"

Farnham now hesitated, realizing he had opened his mouth a little too wide. He was aware that both Lassiter and Mitchell were watching, awaiting his answer, and that he would have little chance of sidestepping the issue now.

"Well, just what did Markham have to say to you?" he asked Lassiter, hoping that by turning the tables he might not appear so defensive. "You know, he doesn't want me elected and he's been spreading rumors. I wouldn't believe anything he might have told you, if I were you."

"I'll tell you just what he said," Lassiter said evenly. "He said he has solid evidence that you are tied in with the Ming Chins and that you've decided to make that group stronger by taking over territory now occupied by the Ta Kuos, the group that came in here tonight. I don't know what to believe, but I would hate to think that was true."

Farnham now grew quite indignant. "How dare you accuse me of something like that!" he shot out. "You're just a saddle tramp and you come in here telling me all this. Who do you think you are, anyway?"

"I was telling you what Markham said," Lassiter told Farnham. His voice was still firm and even, unwavering. "I wasn't accusing you of anything. And I didn't say I agreed or disagreed with Markham. But since you're acting like a kid in trouble on a playground, I'm now beginning to wonder if Markham doesn't have you pegged pretty well."

Farnham opened his mouth to speak and Harold Mitchell interrupted him quickly. "Mr. Farnham," he said, "I've decided I won't have to take any more time to think about whether to go into business with you. There is no question that we have nothing in common. I have no desire to enter into any kind of business venture whatsoever with you. I wish you good luck with your campaign for the city council, but our business connection no longer exists."

Farnham sat forward in his chair, his eyes glaring with rage. "You aren't going to back out on our deal now. No, you're not going to do that."

"We've never had a deal, only a discussion about

possibly entering into one,'' Mitchell corrected him. "We've never even drawn up any papers, much less signed anything. I don't know what you mean by insinuating that I'm backing out on anything."

"I'm just telling you," Farnham said forcefully, "that you'd best go ahead with what we've talked about. It's either that or find yourself in a bad situation."

"Tell us about this 'bad situation' and what that means," Lassiter said to Farnham. "I'd like to hear about that." Nobody said anything, and Lassiter pressed Farnham further. "It isn't very mannerly to try to push people into business deals, and Mr. Mitchell is the last person you'll ever get to do business that way."

"Who are you, anyway," Farnham demanded of Lassiter.

"Let's just say I am to Mr. Mitchell, here, what those two men with you are to you," Lassiter retorted. "How does that sound?"

Farnham leaned back, unable to take Lassiter's glare. When Farnham finally turned away, Lassiter looked to both of the men with Farnham, one of whom met Lassiter's stare. The man then sat forward and pulled the tail of his coat back, exposing a big Colt pistol that rested lightly in a holster across the front of his left hip.

"You don't have very good manners, do you?" the man remarked to Lassiter.

Lassiter almost smiled. This man wanted to impress everyone that he could mean trouble. Lassiter decided to see right then and there what he was made of.

"You'd better be careful, or you'll get your fingers caught in the buttons of that fancy coat," Lassiter told him. "Then manners won't mean a thing and you won't be able to go for your gun. That's what you intended, isn't it?"

The man was silent. He was being pushed hard by

Lassiter, but his instincts were telling him his life would be in danger should he confront this iron-willed gunfighter. He looked to Farnham and the other bodyguard for support, but no one moved.

Lassiter could feel the uncertainty building in all three men. The two bodyguards had certainly never been forced into proving their worth as gunmen and were being made to back down. They were now on the verge of fear, both of them, thinking that they were now up against someone who was stronger than either of them, certainly, and likely could take all *three* of them, Farnham included, if need be. Neither of them had ever had to face a man who was more eager to use a gun than they were.

The bodyguard who had spoken to Lassiter began to fidgit in his chair.

"I asked you a question," Lassiter continued to press. "Do you intend to use that gun?"

Lassiter waited for the man to make some kind of move. He didn't. "No," he finally said. "Just didn't want to take any chances, that's all."

"It seems to me you took a big chance," Lassiter told him. "So, I guess it's understood that Mr. Mitchell is no longer interested in dealing with Mr. Farnham."

Lassiter and Harold Mitchell waited for any one of the three to say or do something. Farnham sat silently, looking at the table, fuming with rage.

Lassiter finally turned to Harold Mitchell. "Do you have any more business here?"

"It's time we joined Lanna," Mitchell said. He got up from his chair and turned without so much as another word to Farnham.

Lassiter followed Mitchell across the ballroom, feeling the intense anger of the three men as they glared after them. Farnham and the other two had heard in no uncertain terms that their world was always going to be separate from Harold Mitchell's. But Lassiter felt quite clearly that before Farnham gave up on ever seeing Harold Mitchell again, those two worlds would certainly collide. And that would happen very soon.

Lassiter sat with Lanna and her father in the dining room once again. They had the whole place nearly to themselves, and the waiters were still very nervous. There were more security people now, many of them deputies, and they watched all the doors carefully.

Lassiter hoped that this time he would be able to finish his meal without interruption. He decided on the duck again, while Harold Mitchell ordered brandy for Lanna and a bottle of whiskey for himself and Lassiter to share.

When another plate of duck arrived, Lassiter began his meal without hesitation.

"How can you have an appetite after all that has happened?" Lanna wanted to know.

"Cast-iron stomach," Lassiter replied. "And besides, it's real empty."

Lanna watched him dissect the duck carefully and begin eating, obviously enjoying himself, yet well-mannered in his dining habits. It was obvious to her that he hadn't enjoyed a good meal in some time. Now he intended to take advantage of the fact that there was a lot of good food available to him.

She watched Lassiter continue to eat and her father think. The two men were silent. Finally, she decided to see how the conversation had gone with L. T. Farnham. She addressed her father in ironic terms.

"From the depth of your thought, can I assume you've decided that Farnham isn't a good business risk?"

"You may assume that," he said, sipping whiskey, "for it is a correct assumption. I must congratulate you on your astuteness, my dear." He caught Lanna's smile and added, "You needn't worry any longer about any association with him. I told him as much, and he became quite *indignant.*"

"That man thinks he owns the world," Lanna said. "You shouldn't have been so eager to go into business with him right away."

Mitchell nodded again, acknowledging his daughter's reprimand. He was ordinarily quite cautious about business affairs and partnerships, and now he realized he had been overanxious to become attached to someone who looked to be headed into the higher realms of political power.

"I had a lot of visions," Mitchell told Lanna honestly. "I guess I've learned something from that, even at my age. But now I have to worry about Farnham cooling down."

"I wouldn't worry about what he said," Lassiter told Mitchell. "Farnham's used to intimidating people when he wants something. It just didn't work for him this time. He'll just have to forget the whole thing, that's all."

"That's what concerns me," Mitchell said. "Will he just forget it? I don't think so."

"You and Lanna will be gone from here in just a matter of hours," Lassiter pointed out. "Farnham's got enough problems tonight to keep him occupied. He'll use his time worrying about the hatchet gang, the Ta Kuos. They'll be after him again, you can bet on it, and they might be waiting for him when he gets home."

Mitchell took a deep breath. "I hope you're right," he told Lassiter. "I've got enough new things on my mind without having Farnham and his threats to complicate things."

"You have other things concerning you, Father?" Lanna asked.

"I'm wondering about that town, Creosote Pass," he told her. "I'm wondering if it would be a good investment after all, that maybe we should proceed with our plans and look into it."

Lanna leaned toward him. "Father, you can't be serious."

"Why not? If there's to be a railroad spur built out there, why wouldn't that town be a sound investment?"

"What about L. T. Farnham?" she asked. "You just said you're worried about him, and now you're talking about fighting him for that little desert rathole."

"He hasn't the ability to go out there and develop anything on his own," Mitchell said. "That's why he wanted me. He isn't the kind of man who's going to do something like that, even if his bid for the city council is a failure."

"He could send somebody else," Lassiter pointed out. "What if he finds somebody like yourself who would want to do the legwork and live out there?"

Mitchell shrugged. "I can't see anybody as real competition. I know how to develop new locations, and do it quickly. There aren't many men, if any, with whom Farnham is acquainted that have the know-how to get a little town going in a hurry."

Lassiter stopped his eating and thought for a moment. "I guess I would have to agree that Farnham wouldn't try to develop Creosote Pass on his own," he finally said. "But it wouldn't surprise me if he would come in later and try to take things over from someone who had already put the work in."

Mitchell nodded. "I suspect that wouldn't bother him at all. But the Nevada desert is a long way from here and he would have to find somebody who would stay out there and look after his interests."

"Then aren't you saying we would have to live out there to look after our interests, if you developed the town?" Lanna then asked.

Mitchell cleared his throat. "Yes, that's a good point, Lanna. But I know some young gentlemen from the city here who wouldn't mind joint ownership in a bank and some other business ventures. If Creosote Pass is worth it, I don't see any problem in getting the development done and finding others to go into partnership with."

Lanna had now sipped her way through three glasses of brandy. She had been in a number of arguments with her father before about his expansion plans throughout the West. Before, he had always managed to convince her that his ideas were sound. But tonight she was determined to hold her ground and win the argument.

"Father, it doesn't seem to me that there is any sense in developing a town so far away from everything," she began. "That's taking a big risk."

"You're missing the point," he argued. "You see, if the railroad builds a spur line, then the town won't be away from everything. It will be a major stopover in the middle of the desert. And people pay for things in the middle of the desert, believe me."

"What about Farnham?" Lassiter put in. "What if he really is serious about wanting to get his own interests developed out there?"

"I'm merely saying that we've got the jump on him and that everything takes time," Mitchell answered. "I suggest we take the train out into that country as far as Reno and ride out to get a look at Creosote Pass. It might be worth developing or it might not. But it wouldn't hurt to look."

Lanna could see her argument slipping away again, despite the fact that Lassiter seemed to be siding with her. "Always wanting to try something new, aren't you, Father?" she commented, with a hint of disgust in her voice. "As if there isn't enough going on with your interests in Glitter Creek now."

"Yes, but it never hurts to look ahead," Mitchell told his daughter. "The gold in Glitter Creek cannot last forever."

"But why must you always be looking for the next big target?" Lanna asked him. "Haven't you got enough money as it is? Why can't you just settle back now and enjoy it?"

Harold Mitchell cleared his throat. He looked at his daughter and gave her an honest appraisal of himself. "Lanna, I'm not the kind of man who can relax, you know that. I've never rested a day in my life and I wouldn't know how to start. You'll have to admit that I keep up a pretty good pace for my age, too."

"That's what concerns me," Lanna told him. "You go too fast. You'll never slow down until something slows you down. And you know if you keep it up, your health will suffer sooner or later. It's bound to."

"Ah! That's nonsense, Lanna," he argued. "My pace is what keeps my health intact. If I tried to slow down, I'd stop completely."

Lanna turned to Lassiter. "You tell him. He won't listen to me."

Lassiter chuckled. "I always stay out of family squabbles. That's my policy. I plan to live a long time, myself, and I don't want people coming at me from both sides."

Lanna turned back to her father. "You just go ahead then and develop all the towns you can find. Then when they're all going at once, you'll worry yourself to death about what's happening in each one. You can't run fast enough to be in all of them at the same time."

"You've really got yourself worked up, haven't you?" Mitchell said with a laugh. "Now I'm beginning to worry about *your* health. You'll worry yourself to death over me." He laughed again and winked at Lassiter.

"I just think it's time you slowed down," Lanna said. "There's no reason to work so hard. No reason at all."

"Well, maybe that's true," Harold Mitchell told his

daughter after some thought. "But I want to see what that little town out there in the desert looks like first. For some reason, I think it's real important, no matter what happens."

"No matter what happens, Father?" Lanna said.

Harold Mitchell nodded. "No matter what happens."

6

LANNA REALIZED she wasn't going to get anywhere with her argument, no matter how sound she might think it was. Her father was never going to stop looking for the next opportunity as long as he lived. She had discussed this with him on many occasions—always with the same results. She just hoped something didn't happen to him that would make him slow down. Then it might be too late.

And now he was intent on traveling across miles of desert to look at Creosote Pass. She could see by the way he was now looking at Lassiter that he would be asking him if he would hire on to go with them.

"Lassiter, how would you like to see the great territory of Nevada," Harold Mitchell then asked.

Lassiter was just finishing his meal. "I was wondering if we wouldn't be getting around to that sooner or later. I don't know that there's anything I've left out there that I want to go back after."

"You know I'll make it well worth your while," Mitchell went on. "In fact, I'll double the salary I gave you in Glitter Creek. What do you say?"

"Say no, Lassiter," Lanna put in. "Then maybe he won't go."

Mitchell turned to her. "I'm going whether or not *anybody* else goes out there with me."

Lanna turned back to Lassiter. "Say yes, Lassiter, please. If he's that stubborn, I'll have to go with him. And I don't want the two of us facing what's out there without you along."

Lassiter looked at Lanna and then at Harold Mitchell. "Double the wages I got in Glitter Creek, eh?"

"Isn't that enough?" Mitchell asked. "I'll pay you more."

"Oh, no," Lassiter said with a chuckle. "I'm not a robber. Twice what I got in Glitter Creek is the most I've ever gotten for any job I've ever been on. I'm just wondering if it's worth it to you to pay me that and also stand the expenses of going all that way into the desert. Maybe there's nothing there. You stand the risk of spending a lot of money."

"But maybe there is," Mitchell insisted. "That's how you have to look at it. You have to think positive. You can't say 'nothing' is out there."

"You've never been out in that desert before, have you?" Lassiter said. "If you had, you'd understand what 'nothing' really means. That part of the country gives a broad new scope to the word."

"See?" Lanna told her father. "Now will you understand that there are some parts of this world that are just not suited for your plans?"

Mitchell laughed again and sipped on another whiskey. "Well," he finally said, "I still want to give it a try."

Lanna had already known what he was going to say and was already looking the other way.

"I really want to hire you to accompany us, Lassiter," Mitchell continued. "What do you say?"

"I wasn't doing anything for a while this spring

anyway," Lassiter finally said. "I'll take you up on it."

Though Lanna was disturbed at not having won the argument, she breathed a sigh of relief at hearing Lassiter's commitment to go with them. She watched her father laugh and shake Lassiter's hand.

"I knew you'd accept," he said gleefully. "We're bound to find something out there."

"Don't count on it," Lassiter said. "Unless you're talking about horned toads and rattlesnakes."

"Just think of it this way," Mitchell said. "If we don't find anything, we can just say we've been on vacation. How's that sound?"

"Vacation?" Lanna questioned.

Mitchell laughed again. "I'm sorry you don't find that amusing, Lanna," he said. "That's a part of the country we've never been to. Lot's of sun, you know."

"Very well, Father," Lanna said, blowing out her breath. "I can see we'll be getting some desert sunshine before too much longer. So if you'll excuse me, I'll retire for the night."

Lassiter and Lanna's father both rose from their chairs. Lanna told Lassiter she would see him in the morning and hoped her father could wait to get to Creosote Pass long enough to have breakfast with them.

"I'll accompany you upstairs," Mitchell said quickly, smiling at his daughter's own sense of humor. He then looked to Lassiter. "We can continue this discussion at breakfast. I bid you good evening."

When they were gone, Lassiter sat back down to have the slice of fresh peach pie that the waiter brought. He was enjoying the dessert when Harold Mitchell returned and sat down. He obviously had something he wanted to discuss that just couldn't wait until breakfast.

"You sure are excited about this trip into the desert," Lassiter chaffed him. "Are you going to tell me that you want to leave tonight?"

"No, I just wanted to discuss the project with you without Lanna's interruption," he replied. "It might not be fair, but I feel we can get so much more done in her absence."

"She just doesn't want you to go," Lassiter commented in her defense.

"Don't misunderstand me, I'm not attacking her," Mitchell said. "But she just doesn't understand me when it comes to business."

"Maybe she understands you all too well," Lassiter suggested.

Mitchell nodded slightly and sipped his whiskey. "Perhaps she does, at that. But I can't help who I am, and if Creosote Pass has anything at all to offer, I feel that it would be foolish to pass it up."

"You couldn't convince me one way or the other," Lassiter said, finishing his pie. "But I've hired on to go with you and I'll stay with you and Lanna for as long as it takes to make your decision."

"I appreciate that," Mitchell said. "I've already seen to it that your horse will be cared for. This establishment offers one of the best stables and boarding facilities in the entire city. Your horse will receive the finest care."

"I appreciate that," Lassiter said. "That was one of my main concerns."

Mitchell was nodding when one of the hotel security men ran up to the table, out of breath.

"Mr. Mitchell! It's your daughter!" he gasped. "A hatchet gang has broken into her room. They're trying to get her out of the hotel now."

Lassiter was up from his seat and had his twin Colts drawn before he had taken one step. He could already hear yelling and shooting, and he rushed from the dining room and into the grand court. Hotel guests were again running for cover everywhere. Hatchet men were spreading out along the different tiers of the hotel.

This gang was not dressed in red, but black. Lassiter recognized them as his old friends from earlier that day—the Ming Chins.

Lassiter thought about Farnham. This was the group he was affiliated with. Farnham hadn't wasted any time in making good on his threat of getting back at Harold Mitchell. Taking Lanna would give him a lot of leverage.

Three gang members held Lanna fast as they descended to the first floor in one of the rising rooms. Lassiter could see that her hands were tied behind her and that a scarf had been tied across her mouth. The rising room had descended past the third level and was making its way down.

Two security men had already fallen and two others were exchanging fire with the other gang members, who had taken position on various levels of the hotel, clearing the way for the three with Lanna. Lassiter could see they had planned things well and that it was going to be difficult to get Lanna away from them.

Lassiter dodged behind a marble pillar as gang members began firing at him. Harold Mitchell ran out to yell when he saw Lanna being held in the rising room. But Lassiter quickly pulled him behind a support column. Bullets poured down at them from gang members positioned along the tiers above them.

"You stay behind cover here and don't move," Lassiter ordered Mitchell. "You won't do Lanna any good with a bullet in you."

"I can't let them take her!" he yelled in anguish. "I can't let that happen!"

"I'll get her back," Lassiter promised. "You just stay here, like I said."

Lassiter eased out from behind the column and fired at a gang member who was slinking along the tier just above him. The man spun a half-circle, dropping his pistol over the ledge as he fell backward into a support column.

Moving quickly, Lassiter retrieved the pistol and slid it along the floor to Harold Mitchell.

"Use it if you have to," Lassiter told him, "but don't move from your position."

Two more hatchet men appeared on the third level. Lassiter dodged their bullets, then fired quickly, hitting one high in the right shoulder. The wounded man yelled and fell back out of sight.

The other gang member took two bullets through the upper chest. He tried to steady himself, but tumbled down off the third level, screaming until the marble floor stopped his fall.

Lassiter continued to move toward the rising room, keeping himself behind the pillars as best he could. The Ming Chins had retreated for the most part, unwilling to risk any more of their members to Lassiter's guns.

But the three who were taking Lanna stayed with her. The one with the large hatchet raised it over her head as they stepped out of the rising room. Lassiter knew he had no chance to stop them, for if he even was able to shoot two of them quickly, the third would kill Lanna before Lassiter's guns could stop him.

Lanna's abductors shot at Lassiter and any others who were in sight as they dragged Lanna out the front and pushed her up on a horse, where she was forcibly held in front of one of their members. Lassiter had no way to get to them, as more Ming Chins came out of the shadows to support the getaway. These members, and others who rode around them, shielded them from the rush of sheriff's deputies that were converging on the scene.

Lassiter managed to get a shot off at one of the last of the Ming Chins, knocking him from his horse. After reloading, Lassiter didn't wait for any of the deputies but instead caught the horse and rode after the Ming Chins toward Chinatown.

Some of the gang spun around to face him. Lassiter charged the horse toward them, knowing they weren't accustomed to fighting like this, especially against someone who had had a great deal of experience with a gun.

Two more of the Ming Chins fell to the street before a bullet plunged into Lassiter's mount, staggering the animal to its knees. Lassiter jumped down and sprinted, keeping his eyes on the horsemen galloping away. But soon they were gone and only the shadows at the edge of Chinatown remained.

This was no time to slow down, Lassiter realized. He had no idea where the Ming Chins were taking Lanna or what they intended to do with her. But they would have to take her someplace to hold her, and he would have to find that place as soon as he could.

Lassiter reloaded once again and hurried into the middle of Chinatown. He stepped over hopheads unconscious from opium and studied the alleys and stairwells for any signs of hatchet men dressed in black.

It seemed impossible to even think of finding her in the congestion of shadowed night life. None of the local inhabitants would even think of talking to him. People scurried out of his way, and members of other hatchet gangs watched him carefully as he wound his way along the Dupont Gai and finally onto Jackson Street.

Lassiter finally realized that he was too visible, far too visible, and that as long as he was seen there would be little chance of his locating Lanna. He finally resigned himself to patience and slipped into an alley to wait until the streets got back to normal.

He stood for a while, breathing the dank air and allowing his eyes to grow accustomed to the dark. The alley was thick with filth and litter. He stood motionless, blending into his surroundings, while rats scurried at his feet. He had lodged himself into a corner, and after a little while longer, even the hopheads began to come and go without noticing him.

At last he heard a woman crying out and fighting desperately as two men dragged her up a stairwell from a basement at the far end of the alley. At the top of the stairwell a red lantern burned and in its light, Lassiter could see that the woman was a small Oriental, and that the men were dressed in black.

He had found the Ming Chins.

Lassiter concluded they were taking the woman to the waterfront: the woman was being shanghaied. Since they were Ming Chins, there was a better than even chance that Lanna was down below, where they had brought the woman from.

Lassiter pondered his situation a moment. He could go right to the stairwell and take his chances on finding Lanna, or he could wait and find out from the woman and the Ming Chins. If he decided to just go down into the den on his own, he could lose precious time if Lanna wasn't down there. He decided it would be best to wait for the two Ming Chins and the woman. That way he could be sure.

The woman continued to fight as the two Ming Chins hauled her down the alley toward Lassiter. Even though her hands were tied behind her back, she kicked and spat at them. She was fighting them valiantly, but had no chance of escape.

They reached Lassiter and he stepped quickly out of the shadows and pistol-whipped the Ming Chin closest to him. He released the woman and slumped to the ground. Before the other Ming Chin had time to react, Lassiter had jammed his pistol into the man's middle.

"Let the girl go," Lassiter growled.

The gang member hesitated, but Lassiter was not to be denied. He again ordered the gang member to release the girl. He didn't want to kill the Ming Chin if he could help it, for the gang member could be his ticket down into the den where Lanna might still be held. But he had to hurry, for he realized the longer it took him to look for Lanna, the less chance he would have of locating her. He could only hope that they hadn't taken her out already.

7

THE MING CHIN shook his head and held the woman all the tighter. Lassiter realized the gang member would rather face death than have the woman taken from him.

Lassiter quickly brought the pistol up and clubbed the Ming Chin. He dropped to the ground, unconscious, beside his comrade. The woman, now freed, gasped and tried to run. But Lassiter quickly caught her.

She kicked and screamed as she had with the two Ming Chins, until Lassiter finally wrapped a big arm around her tightly. She tilted her face up to his, her eyes wide and filled with fear.

"Don't be afraid of me," Lassiter told her. "I won't hurt you. I just want to ask you a question or two. Then I'll let you go. But you have to help me first."

"Help you?" she said weakly.

Lassiter was relieved to know that she did understand English. A thick fog was beginning to settle in over town, but in the dim reddish glow of the lamp at the end of the alley, Lassiter could see that she was not entirely Oriental—she was part Caucasian.

"Can't help you," she said and tried to squirm loose.

Lassiter continued to hold her fast. "Please, I'm not going to hurt you," he told her again. To emphasize the point, he pulled his bandanna off from around his neck and wiped some of the blood from her mouth and face. "Friend," he said. "I'm your friend."

She seemed to relax. But he continued to grasp her tightly. He couldn't afford to lose his only chance to learn where Lanna was being held.

"I need your help," Lassiter again told her. "I helped you, now you help me. Understand?"

"What you want?" she finally asked.

"Those men are Ming Chins," Lassiter said, pointing to the two unconscious gang members. "I want to know if—"

"Ming Chins," she interrupted him, struggling in his grasp. "Shanghai . . . shanghai . . ."

Lassiter held her tightly again until she settled down.

"Please," Lassiter pleaded again. "I don't want to harm you. I want to know about a woman. She has red hair. Woman. Red hair."

Lassiter noticed how she quickly looked over toward the stairwell. The fog had almost obscured the light—it was now but a dim and hazy reddish glow. He pointed over.

"There? Woman with red hair? Over there?"

She nodded. "Ming Chins take her. She with me. Shanghai."

Lassiter froze. Was she saying they had taken Lanna away already, or that they intended to?

"Is she down there now?" Lassiter asked her. "Woman with red hair, down there now? Or did they already take her?"

"Ming Chins there," she answered. "Red-haired woman still down there."

She struggled to free herself again and this time Lassiter let her go and watched her flee the alley. In a few moments she was lost in the fog.

With new hope, Lassiter hurried toward the dim red lamp over the stairwell. With both pistols ready, he hurried down the steps and stopped in front of a rickety wooden door.

He could hear very little besides muffled voices coming from within, but he felt very sure now that Lanna was in there, somewhere, in the maze of tunnels that led under the city. If he could get her out, they would have a chance to escape in the fog.

Lassiter burst through the door and leveled both guns. Startled people gasped. He found himself in a brothel, where mostly white men were lounging with Oriental women. The air was sultry and oppressive, thick with smoke from pots and dimly lit by the yellow haze of opium lamps that hung in various locations.

It took a moment or two for the brothel patrons to recover from their surprise. When they did, some of them jumped up and ran out past Lassiter. Others—their senses distorted by drug—either laughed or lay complacently. An old Oriental woman spewed anger at him in Chinese and took a long, curved knife from under a counter. But she was too afraid of him to move closer.

Lassiter ignored the old woman and headed toward the back without hesitation, pushing through a curtain of hanging bamboo stems. He was met by two more Ming Chins, both of whom carried large clubs. They literally ran into Lassiter coming through another curtain.

One of them quickly raised his club. Lassiter jammed the barrel of his Colt into the man's abdomen and fired.

The explosion was muffled, but the bullet ripped a

large hole through the Ming Chin's middle, spraying the wall behind him with blood and body tissue. He dropped to the floor and kicked a few times before he lay still.

Lassiter saw that the second Ming Chin was primarily of Caucasian blood, at least three-quarters, and could tell as he told him to raise his hands that he was the same man who had led the gang members out into the street in front of him when he had first ridden into town.

"I knew we should have killed you," the big Ming Chin said. "A mistake I knew I would pay for."

Lassiter watched him as he seemed to contemplate going for a pistol on his belt. Lassiter leveled both Colts at his midsection.

"Go right ahead," Lassiter challenged. "You'll end up just like your friend on the floor."

The big man held his hand frozen for a moment, then moved it back away from the pistol. Lassiter stepped forward and took the piece, along with a knife, and jammed them both down into his own belt. Lassiter then ordered the big Ming Chin to the floor—onto his stomach, with his hands behind his head.

"You won't make it out alive," the Ming Chin promised.

Lassiter ignored him and kept the man down by pointing the pistol at his head. He could hear the old woman coming up from behind and turned just in time with his other pistol as she started to raise the curved knife.

"Tell her to drop the knife," Lassiter ordered the Ming Chin on the floor, "or she'll end up like the other one here."

The Ming Chin was silent and Lassiter stomped a boot into the small of his back.

"Do what I tell you, or you'll see her die."

The big Ming Chin told the woman in Chinese that

the gunfighter wanted to kill her and would if she didn't drop the knife.

"Ahhh! No! No!" Her breath was ragged and her face was contorted with fear.

Lassiter continued to hold the pistol in his right hand on her. She wasn't going to move. She was frozen with fear, the knife clenched between her fingers.

Lassiter then ordered the big Ming Chin on the floor to tell her that she would not die if she dropped the knife, but that she would if she continued to hold it. Then he wanted her to lie down on her stomach, with her hands behind her head, or he was going to end her life right then and there.

The Ming Chin translated the order, and finally, the old woman dropped the knife and did as she was told. Lassiter then knelt down next to the Ming Chin and looked hard at him, holding one of the pistols near the man's ear.

"Do you know where the redheaded woman is?" he asked. "Harold Mitchell's daughter?"

There was no answer. The Ming Chin only shrugged.

Lassiter then put the barrel of his Colt right into the man's ear.

"No one will hear this. You ready?"

"No, wait!" he said quickly. "She's in one of the rooms. Back in the tunnels."

"Which room?"

"I wasn't in there. I just saw them take her back."

"Did they take her out again?"

The big Ming Chin shook his head. "Not unless they went the other way."

"Good," Lassiter said. "You're my ticket back into that rathole. You can show me around. You're going to walk in front of me. And if there's any problems, you'll never see the light of day again. Understand?"

Lassiter backed off him slowly and pulled the Ming

Chin to his feet by his long queue. When he was up, Lassiter let go of his hair and the Ming Chin stepped back, eyeing Lassiter's gun. He was well aware by now that Lassiter would use it if he didn't cooperate, and wasn't about to try and make a break. He just nodded as Lassiter motioned for him to lead the way out the back of the brothel and into the tunnels.

With the Ming Chin in front of him and past yet another door, Lassiter found himself in a narrow interior. It was a long tunnel, also dank and dimly lit with opium lamps, which led past a series of small cubicle rooms. He would have to search each room in turn.

Knowing he had no time to waste, Lassiter pushed the Ming Chin ahead of him down the tunnel, looking into the rooms as he passed them. It was hard to see into the smoky cubicles, and in the process of looking for Lanna he disturbed a lot of naked people. He just hoped he wouldn't find them using her in one of the rooms.

"You'd better get out while you can," the Caucasian Ming Chin spoke up. "There's a lot of us and you'll never make it alive."

"No, I'm not letting you go," Lassiter told him calmly. "You're in the same position you were earlier today out on the street. When the shooting starts, you'll be the first to go."

Lassiter pushed the Ming Chin ahead. He took hold of the gang member's queue and held it tightly. It would be the best way to control him. The Ming Chin complained bitterly.

"What's that for? Let go of me. I ain't going to go nowhere."

"There's not many rooms left," Lassiter told him. "And she'd better be down here. Otherwise, I'll take this pigtail of yours back with me. And it will be attached to the rest of your scalp. I could trade it to the Indians for a nice buffalo robe."

The Ming Chin grunted and said no more. Lassiter

eased him ahead, and they continued. Finally, as they got ever deeper into the tunnel, he could hear a woman's voice he recognized as Lanna's.

She was shouting something, likely venting her anger at being abducted. Lassiter could feel the Ming Chin tensing up and pulled all the tighter on his queue, bringing his head back farther so that he could not see that well ahead of him.

"Let's go slow," Lassiter ordered. "Real slow. You do your part, and I won't kill you. Understood?"

The Ming Chin nodded. Lassiter kicked the door in and stood with his gun trained on two Ming Chins, who were tightening a blindfold around Lanna's eyes. There was another man—an Oriental who was not much more than a boy—who was already blindfolded. Like Lanna, he was on his knees, and remained there, rigidly still.

Though she couldn't see, Lanna could tell immediately that it was Lassiter.

"Thank God you've come," she gasped.

The two Ming Chins were still standing near Lanna and Lassiter pulled on the big man's queue and told him to order the two men to the floor, with their hands behind their heads.

"You'd better tell them quick," Lassiter told the big Ming Chin, "or I might think you told them something else and have to blow your head off."

The Caucasion Ming Chin spoke hurriedly in Chinese to the other two gang members, and they went to the floor immediately. Dragging the Ming Chin with him, Lassiter eased over and worked Lanna's blindfold off. Then, using the Ming Chin's knife, he cut her bonds.

"I was beginning to think I'd never see you or my father again," she said. Tears popped up in her eyes.

"We've got to get out of here first," Lassiter pointed out. "But finding you was a big step."

Lanna looked to the young Chinese prisoner. "This

young man can help us," she said. "He knows a good way out of here."

"I can help, yes," the young man said. "Take me with and I lead you out."

"Free him then," Lassiter told Lanna, handing her the knife. "We're running out of time."

Lanna hurriedly freed the young man and gave Lassiter back the knife. He smiled at Lanna and Lassiter.

"Cheng Li," he said. "My name Cheng Li. Just Lee most of time."

"I heard them calling him Lee," Lanna said. "He used to work for Farnham. I don't know what he did."

"If he can help us out of here, then I think we'd better take him," Lassiter said, as he continued to hold the big Ming Chin by the hair. "It's not a good idea to go back the way I got in here."

"I take you good way," Lee said, bowing to Lassiter. He smiled and then turned and looked contemptuously at the Ming Chins. He pointed to the knife Lanna still held in her hand.

"I will kill them." He made a motion across his own throat. "Not follow us."

Lassiter felt the big Caucasian Ming Chin begin to tense again. He began to struggle and Lassiter had to hold his pistol in the man's neck to settle him down.

"You told me you wouldn't kill me," he told Lassiter angrily.

"Just relax," Lassiter said. "You're not dead yet. But don't push it."

"We'll tie them up," Lassiter told Lee. "If they think we're going to kill them anyway, they'll be trouble. There'll be more of the gang here soon enough as it is."

Lee again bowed to Lassiter. Lassiter had the Caucasian Ming Chin lie down next to the other two, and he and Lee tied them securely, then gathered up the scarves and pieces of cloth in the room to gag them with.

"You should thank me for not giving him the knife," Lassiter told the big Caucasian Ming Chin as he prepared to put a length of red cloth around his mouth and face.

The Ming Chin grunted. "You can't go far enough that we won't find you."

Lassiter clamped the cloth tight through the Ming Chin's mouth, making him groan. He then rose and with Lee and Lanna started for the door.

Lanna and Lee had taken pistols from the gang members for themselves on the way out of the tunnel. Lassiter knew that Lanna could handle a pistol; he asked Lee if he knew how to shoot.

Lee tilted a big Colt Army .44 sideways. "Just point end and pull on little piece of metal." He started to pull the trigger.

Lassiter grabbed the pistol and pointed it toward the floor. "That's right, Lee. But not now."

Lanna was looking at Lassiter and her eyes were wide. "He doesn't hesitate to try things, I know that. He's lucky he's still alive."

Lassiter nodded and turned to Lee. "Don't shoot this gun, not unless you absolutely have to. Understand?"

"Sound good," Lee said. "It heavy." He tried to tuck it into his belt, pulling on the trigger again as he worked.

"Better yet, I'll give it back to you if you need it," Lassiter suggested, taking the pistol from Lee and tucking it into his own belt. "You just lead the way out of here and hope we don't run into more Ming Chins."

Lee took them from the room back into the tunnel and down to where another tunnel split off to the right. Behind them, they could hear the sounds of men yelling in Chinese.

"Where does this go?" Lassiter asked Lee.

"Don't know," Lee said.

"I thought you knew how to get us out of here," Lassiter said with annoyance.

"You want *safe* way out, don't you?" Lee asked. "Don't know if there is safe way out."

"We had better get going somewhere," Lanna then suggested. "I can hear them coming a lot closer to us all the time."

They ran down the tunnel a ways and Lee stopped them and pointed to another tunnel that branched off.

"Know that way out," Lee said. "But that lead to where Ta Kuos keep women. Ta Kuos worse than Ming Chins."

Lassiter remembered it was the Ta Kuos who had first come into the hotel and had killed and wounded so many dignitaries. He knew they would remember him if he showed up in one of their opium dens. But the Ming Chins were closing swiftly from behind. They had no choice but to go forward.

8

THEY HURRIED THROUGH THE TUNNEL, through layers of opium smoke that seemed to grow ever thicker. It was a maze that, on their own, would have made Lassiter and Lanna hopelessly lost. With Lee showing the way, they made good time and avoided being caught by the pursuing Ming Chins.

But they were now in Ta Kuo territory and their danger was just as great.

They passed two tunnels where men dressed in red—Ta Kuos—were hauling women toward the top. One of them, the Ta Kuo lieutenant who had sworn the oath at Lassiter after the shootout in the hotel, saw Lassiter and hurried ahead and into the darkness.

"That could mean real trouble," Lassiter said. "He's bound to warn the others."

They saw no more Ta Kuos for a time. And they knew the Ming Chins wouldn't invade this part of the tunnels, not without a lot of men and a good reason to risk lives. Lee said they were nearing the place where they could get out and that their chances were good of escaping in the fog outside.

Everything seemed to be falling into place. But the heavy smoke was finally beginning to get to Lanna.

"How much farther?" she asked. "I'm beginning to feel light-headed."

Lee turned to her and chuckled. "You not good smoker. You be easy hophead."

"I wouldn't be an easy hophead," Lanna said defensively. "I'm just starting to get a headache, that's all. I thought the stuff was supposed to make you forget your troubles."

"Some people think this," Lee said. "Truth is, it the beginning of your troubles. Many bad dreams. Dragons come and burn you."

"You've had the experience?" Lassiter asked him.

"As a child," Lee said with a nod. "It given to me by my mother. I ran away."

"That's brave of you, Lee, to be able to get away from this as a child," Lanna said. "How much farther until we're back up on top?"

Lee stopped them and looked down a short tunnel. He saw in the shadows where a rickety set of wooden stairs led upward to a door.

"There!" he said. "I found it. That the way out where Ta Kuos come and go."

They hurried into the short tunnel and were almost to the steps when the door opened. A number of Ta Kuos poured in, but stopped abruptly when they saw Lassiter pushing Lanna and Lee behind him.

"Big trouble!" Lee said. He reached for the pistol Lassiter had in his belt.

Lassiter pulled the big Colt and told Lee just to hold it and not to fire, unless he absolutely had to. Then he pulled both of his own Colts.

The Ta Kuos were trapped by the stairs and though five of them had already burst through and were pulling weapons, they had no chance against Lassiter, whose black-handled Colts spit fire into the dank and smutty air.

As Lassiter's bullets riddled their bodies, Ta Kuos fell off one another and against the sooty walls of the tunnel. One of them managed to pull off a wild shot before going down under Lassiter's hail of gunfire. The bullet smashed into an opium pot, blowing out cinders of burning drug that flew like sparks from a fireworks display.

Other Ta Kuos who had started to come through the door now escaped back up and quickly closed it. Lassiter then turned as he heard Lanna and Lee yelling for him from behind. Lee began firing the pistol and Lassiter joined them as a host of black-clad Ming Chins started into the small tunnel. Despite the danger, the Ming Chins had continued after them.

The Ming Chins retreated before Lee's wild shooting. Lee had somehow hit one of them. The wounded gang member was crawling along the tunnel floor, calling for his comrades to get him. Lassiter hurriedly reloaded, realizing they had to get out of the tunnel right away or be trapped by the Ming Chins when they regrouped and returned.

Lassiter led the way to the small stairway, then rushed up and kicked the doorjamb to splinters. He fired into three Ta Kuos waiting beside the door, and at moving figures in the fog just ahead of him. He heard men yelling and running through the alley, and realized he had routed the Ta Kuos—for the time being.

Now there were Ming Chins to worry about.

Lassiter then helped Lanna and Lee out of the tunnel. He waited at the door for a short time, looking down the steps into the darkness of the tunnel. When two Ming Chins appeared, he shot them both, then pulled himself out of the opening and with his back against a building, reloaded once again.

The Ming Chins would likely be a lot more cautious now before trying to come up out of the tunnel, Lassiter knew, and it would give them a chance to make their escape from the alley through the fog and out of Chinatown.

They stayed close to the walls of the buildings, moving cautiously, watching closely for Ta Kuos and any Ming Chins that might appear from another entrance to the tunnels. When they had gotten themselves past two more streets, Lassiter stopped them to listen and study the alleys.

"All quiet," Lee said to Lassiter. "You scare hell out of all Chinatown."

Lee continued to marvel at Lassiter's shooting and told him that he believed both tong gangs were not going to take any more chances, especially in the fog. They had already lost far too many of their numbers, and none of the rest of them felt like dying.

But Lassiter was never one to rest easy before he was certain of things.

"We can't say this thing is over yet," he told Lee. "We're still in Chinatown."

"We still in Chinatown," Lee acknowledged, "but for time being, Chinatown belong to you."

"I'm beginning to get the idea that these hatchet gangs play for keeps, and that they don't stop until they get their way," Lassiter said. "Why do you think they've given up?"

"Hatchet gangs, as you call them—tong gangs, as we call them—they very bad men," Lee said. "You right. They not stop until they get their way. But they not get their way with you. Very frightened. You shoot them up good. Very good. Tong gangs never shot up that way before. They maybe think you use magic. They stay back."

"Well, I don't want to give them another chance at us," Lassiter said. "We'd better move on."

"Where you go?" Lee asked.

"Back to the Palace Hotel," Lanna replied. "What is the shortest way back?"

"I lead you back to hotel," Lee said. "Big man in black save my life. I lead you back."

"The big man's name is Lassiter," Lanna told him.

"Las-si-ter?" He looked at Lassiter.

Lassiter nodded. "Yes, Lassiter is the name."

Lee smiled. "Lassiter. That mean, 'big man in black who shoot quick'?"

Lassiter chuckled. "It just means Lassiter."

Lee showed them the shortest way back, through the alleys and along the edges of the streets. The fog helped hide them. In addition, it was getting very late and very few people were out. They would often stumble onto hopheads who didn't know where they were, but almost everyone else was off the streets.

Lanna rushed into her father's arms upon reaching the hotel. Harold Mitchell had just been getting ready to call the marshal back to try to talk him into taking a posse of deputies into Chinatown to look for Lassiter and his daughter. He was relieved to know he wouldn't have to do that.

In the light of the lobby, Lassiter could see that Mitchell had worn himself to a frazzle with worry. His tie was gone and his shirt rumpled and soaked with sweat. He confessed he had not been able to sit still and had paced the lobby nearly the entire time. He looked his daughter over closely.

"Did they harm you in any way, Lanna?" he asked.

"They knew they would have to kill me first," Lanna said. "And they wanted me alive. An old Chinese woman told them not to bother me."

After telling her father the entire story, Lanna introduced Lee to him.

"He showed us the way out of the tunnels and then back here," she said. "I was lucky he was with me."

"I was lucky you with *me*," Lee corrected her. "And we both lucky Lassiter have two big guns."

"He's used them in our behalf before," Mitchell

told Lee. "I doubt if I can ever thank him enough. He always seems to be here when we need him."

Lanna looked to Lee to ask him some questions. She was interested in the welfare of this young man who had risked his life to get them out of the tunnels.

"Do you have to go back to Chinatown again?" she asked him. "Won't you find yourself in the same situation as before?"

"Si . . . tu . . . a . . ." Lee stumbled with the word.

"I mean," Lanna explained, "won't the Ming Chins look for you again?"

"I not go back to Chinatown," Lee said. "No. I not go back there. I go to railroad and jump train out of town. Go a long way away. I not want Farnham to ever find me."

"Farnham?" Lassiter said. "Do you mean L. T. Farnham?"

"L. T. Farnham, yes," Lee said with a nod. "I once work for him. Work for him very long time. Until just yesterday I work for him. Tonight he try to shanghai me."

"Why don't we go someplace where we can talk," Mitchell suggested. "Perhaps in the far end of the dining room, where it's quiet."

They moved out of the lobby and found a secluded corner of the dining room. Harold Mitchell still exhibited his relief at having Lanna back safe and sound. He told Lee more than once that he was grateful for what he had done for Lanna until Lassiter's arrival. All the while, Lassiter was wondering what possible connection this young man could have with L. T. Farnham.

"Would you care for something to drink, Lee?" Mitchell asked Lee when the waiter appeared.

Lee shook his head. "No drink. Make me see funny. No drink."

Harold Mitchell nodded. He ordered brandy for himself and Lassiter. Lanna declined to drink anything more herself. All she wanted now was to get some sleep and try to forget what had taken place. But first she wanted to hear what Lee had to say about his connection with L. T. Farnham.

"Tell us more about Farnham," Lassiter said to Lee. "You said you worked for him for a considerable length of time?"

Lee nodded. "I waiter. I work for him five year, maybe. Since I run away from my mother."

"So you know Farnham and his operations in San Francisco real well then," Lassiter said. "Why did he have you tied up in that room with Lanna?"

"Shanghai," Lee said quickly. "Shanghai and then maybe kill me and throw me off boat. I hear about Golden Dragon and why Farnham want to go to desert."

Lassiter now looked at Harold Mitchell, who was himself becoming more and more interested in the discussion.

"What's this about a golden dragon?" Lassiter asked.

"There a very valuable piece of Chinese sculpture art hidden in desert," Lee went on. "Ten year ago or more, when railroad built, it stolen from homeland, from emperor, and brought in boat to new land. Dragon then hidden somewhere near railroad. For over ten year Golden Dragon hidden in desert and just now Farnham find out about where it might be."

"This Golden Dragon is something very special, then," Lassiter said with a nod. "And I imagine only a very few people know where it might be hidden."

"Yes," Lee said with a quick nod. "Farnham and Ho Yang, the leader of Ming Chins. Old woman in tunnels his wife. Farnham and Ho Yang want to find dragon. It very sacred. Very valuable. Farnham and Ho Yang want to find it and sell it back to emperor in homeland. Big ransom."

Harold Mitchell was nodding. He turned to Lassiter.

"It sounds like Farnham was more interested in that artifact than he ever was in Creosote Pass. He just wanted to use the town as a front to work from."

"And to start an opium trade in," Lassiter added. "He could expand a great deal into a lot of areas with money from an emperor." He then turned back to Lee. "How did you get on Farnham's bad side?"

"I hear Farnham talking to big man, Bard—the one you have as captive when you come into room and find Lanna and myself. He telling Bard that old Chinese man in Nevada, old man who own laundry, have a map that show where dragon buried. Bard see me and tell Farnham. They take me then. They get rid of me so that I not tell anyone. I just glad you find way into tunnels."

"I can hardly believe this," Lanna said. "Farnham isn't content to have a lot of power here in San Francisco. He wants to own everything he sees."

"Well, that means Farnham will likely be going out to Creosote Pass no matter what," Lassiter surmised. "Either that, or he'll send that big man, Bard, to find the dragon for him."

"He send Bard," Lee said with a nod. "Bard do all work for Farnham and Ho Yang."

"It's pretty important that we catch the first train out there in the morning," Mitchell said. "I just want to get a look at Creosote Pass and decide what to do. I don't care about the dragon."

"Why don't we just forget about the whole thing, Father?" Lanna suggested. "Haven't we gotten ourselves in enough trouble already?"

"Maybe if Farnham finds the dragon, he'll forget about us," Harold Mitchell suggested. "That's all he really wants. Besides, it's a matter of principle with me now."

Lanna took a deep breath. "A matter of principle. I'm afraid we're in store for a lot more trouble, just for a matter of principle."

9

L. T. FARNHAM sat smoking a cigar in the dimly lit interior of an underground brothel. It was nearing dawn and the brothel was mostly empty. It had never really refilled since a gunfighter dressed in black had broken in and shot the place to pieces.

Farnham was almost too angry to sit still. He was not used to being made a fool of, and he rarely met with people who used more force than he did in getting their way.

What bothered him most was the fact that Harold Mitchell's daughter was no longer in his custody. And there was no way he was going to get her back now, not tonight. He would certainly have no chance of even getting the Ming Chins to go back after her and her father. Not with that gunfighter watching over them.

Farnham continued to smoke and sulk. He was as of yet in no mood to think of another plan. His two bodyguards could only sit beside him and wait for his orders, whatever they might be. Farnham had a reputation for ordering odd things at odd times.

What the two of them were most afraid of was the possibility that Farnham would order them after this gunfighter. Neither of them liked to think of that taking place, as he had already called them and neither had been able to stand up to him. With the knowledge now of what he had done in Chinatown, both were certain they never wanted to lay eyes on him again.

But they would do what Farnham asked—either that or lose their jobs and risk being killed by new gunmen hired by Farnham who would seek them out and eliminate them, lest they become competition in some way. That was Farnham's way: after you finished working for him, you were finished, period.

L. T. Farnham was having trouble with himself now, though. For the first time in his career, he had failed to get his way. And he certainly didn't like it, nor the thought of the precedent it might set.

But Farnham certainly had no edge on anger in this smoky interior. He, in fact, had to settle for second place in that category.

With Farnham and his bodyguards were two other men: Ho Yang, the leader of the Ming Chins and one of the most powerful figures in Chinatown, and a large man named Bard, who was directly under Ho Yang. Bard was in charge of the hatchet work.

Ho Yang was a distinct figure, with his long, white beard that tapered to a point just above his navel. His face was wrinkled with age and his squinting eyes were nearly hidden. He wore long, tapering emerald earrings and a ring through his left nostril.

There was no one in the room more angry than Ho Yang, and everyone was about to find that out.

But it was the big hatchet man, Bard, who had fallen victim directly to the gunfighter's strength and it was he who spoke up first, and indiscreetly.

"I'll go after him and get him," Bard said confidently. "I'll kill him and then get Mitchell's daughter, like we did before, and we'll have her once and for all."

Ho Yang, who had been stroking his beard and watching Bard with contempt, spoke through a mouth twisted with anger.

"How you plan to do gunfighter in this time, when you have many men before and fail?"

Bard shuffled his feet and looked at the floor. He wasn't yet ready to answer Ho Yang. He would have to think about how he would make up for what had happened and his failure. He didn't want to anger Ho Yang any more deeply.

What made Ho Yang especially formidable—besides being a long-time power among the Ming Chins—was the fact that he could control his anger. Through many years of studying ancient Chinese philosophy and discipline techniques, Ho Yang had developed a strong will and a sensible approach to gaining power for himself.

He was a thinker and when aroused could direct his anger into the right channels and make those around him who had fallen into their own impulsive behavior feel like upstart children.

"A lot of men fall to gunfighter's bullets," Ho Yang continued to rebuke Bard. "You now speak like this man not dangerous, like he nothing at all. You a fool."

"I'll get him," Bard promised. "I'll get it done."

"On your own?" Ho Yang challenged. "You go out on your own? You go out with no men? That how you must do it if you not make plan that I will allow."

Bard's face went hard. "If I have to, I'll go by myself."

Ho Yang laughed out loud. "Who will I choose to take over for you?" Ho Yang asked him. "You never stand up to man in black. Never. He kill you so fast you never see him shoot. You not very smart."

Ho Yang now turned his anger toward Farnham, where he felt it more rightfully belonged.

"Why you want to get involved with this Mitchell in first place?" he asked Farnham. "If you not involved with this Mitchell, gunfighter not be here."

Farnham didn't want to look at Ho Yang, either. He didn't want to face the old man's anger. It wasn't the first time he had been around Ho Yang when the old man was upset, and it wasn't a pleasant experience.

"I need to know why you make foolish choice of business partner?" Ho Yang pressed.

Farnham fought to control his own anger, and the impulse to tell Ho Yang it didn't concern him. But it wasn't smart for him to challenge the old man, for he needed the Ming Chins more badly now than before to protect him against the Ta Kuos and ensure his power within Chinatown.

"Harold Mitchell is good at development," Farnham finally answered. "It would have been real good to have him put together a town out in that desert, so that we could settle in and better get a hold of things out there. It would have made it a lot easier to look for that dragon then."

"Maybe so," Ho Yang acknowledged, "but you didn't say this big man who shoots good was working for Farnham, and that he was at hotel."

"I didn't know anything about this gunfighter," Farnham protested. "He just showed up. He must have been invited by Mitchell. Hell, I don't know."

"That the point," Ho Yang said. "You don't know about gunfighter, then you hear from Mitchell that he not want to do business with you. Then you make bad judgment."

"What bad judgment?"

"You want Mitchell's daughter because you mad at Mitchell," Ho Yang told him, knowing the whole story. "Then gunfighter come to find her and kill a lot of my men. Not good. You should have been smarter. You not need to shanghai his daughter."

Farnham dragged on the cigar and blew smoke into

the air, then clenched his teeth. "I told you, I had no idea about this gunfighter. How was I supposed to know all this would happen?"

"First of all, you lucky he there when Ta Kuos attack," Ho Yang said bluntly. "Then you not tell me about him when I send my men to help you get Mitchell's daughter. If I knew, none of it would have happened. Now a lot of my men killed or hurt. Not good. Ta Kuos can now take us over if we not careful."

"The Ta Kuos lost a lot of men to him, too," Farnham pointed out, his own anger starting to get the best of him. "They're not in much better shape."

At this juncture, Ho Yang's old wife pushed herself through the curtains and bowed respectfully. Ho Yang spoke to her harshly.

"Why you interrupt?"

"Sorry. See men outside. Men listen, I think."

Ho Yang instructed Bard to go with her. Farnham turned to his bodyguards and told them both to go have a look as well. Then Ho Yang started in with Farnham where he had left off.

"The point is," Ho Yang insisted, "we need men to stay powerful. Can't have them killed all time. Have to think."

Farnham knew he was in a hard position. The fact that this gunfighter dressed in black had even showed up as Mitchell's guest had spelled bad luck for him from the beginning. It would have been so easy: Mitchell might never have known that he was tied in with Ho Yang's tong group. And he would likely have already signed a deal to build up the town of Creosote Pass in Nevada Territory.

"So what do we do now?" Farnham asked Ho Yang. "Do we still go into the desert and look for that dragon? Or do we drop the whole thing?"

"That something we must talk about," Ho Yang said. "I learn that Lee, who used to work for you, now with Mitchell and that gunfighter. He will lead them to Golden Dragon and then we have nothing."

Farnham looked quickly at Ho Yang. "I thought your men shanghaied him."

"Gunfighter get there too quick," Ho Yang said. "Lee now with them. He lead them to Golden Dragon."

"Then we've *got* to act fast," Farnham said. "We have to move right away."

"I not so sure now that Golden Dragon all that important to me," Ho Yang told Farnham. "Or that association with you all that important, either."

Farnham at first showed surprise, then got very uncomfortable. "What are you saying?"

"I telling you that to do business with you cost me a lot. I need more of the split we make on deals."

"What?" Farnham asked.

"I make it clear," Ho Yang said. "I want bigger share of ransom from Golden Dragon. You cost me lot of men and lot of time. Now it cost you. I want two-thirds of ransom, not one-half."

Farnham sat up in his chair. "No deal."

"Then we finished, also," Ho Yang said. "Can't do business with a man who push things that can't be pushed. Can't do business with man who make bad decisions. You look for backing from some other tong group." He started to rise from his chair.

"Just a minute, Ho Yang," Farnham said quickly. "Why don't we talk this thing over."

"Nothing to talk over," Ho Yang said, now standing. "I get two-thirds of ransom for dragon, or you can go after dragon on your own and find other tong group. Nothing else to say." He stood for a moment, awaiting Farnham's reaction.

Farnham had no alternative but to accept the terms, however ridiculous. If he broke off with the Ming Chins, Ho Yang certainly wouldn't be a supporter any longer. And Farnham knew that meant he would then be an easy target for another attempt on his life by the Ta Kuos. There was nothing he could do but bow to Ho Yang's wishes.

"You get two-thirds of the ransom, then," Farnham conceded.

Ho Yang sat down again. "We have deal. But I make decisions on how to get Golden Dragon."

"Only if I'm protected from the Ta Kuos here," Farnham objected. "You have to supply all the men who go to Nevada after the dragon. I can't pay men to be here to protect me and men to go out there also. You can better afford that."

Ho Yang bowed his head slightly. "As you wish. I much prefer to send my men, anyway. Your men very afraid of gunfighter. They not worth much."

Ho Yang's wife then came through the curtains once again and bowed. "Men run away. We stay out here and watch."

Ho Yang nodded and the old woman withdrew through the curtains. Farnham sucked on his cigar and sat silent, thinking about what Ho Yang had said about his men being afraid of the gunfighter. It was true; there wasn't any way he could argue that fact. But Ho Yang hadn't seen this man fight.

Ho Yang began his presentation of how the search for the Golden Dragon would take place, and how they would deal with this seasoned gunfighter.

"I make sure all men who go are trained by me, and know what they must face," Ho Yang said. "I have such men, special men. Many in Sacramento. They will know much better how to deal with this gunfighter. And they will know what to do with Lee and how to find the map that shows where Golden Dragon is hidden."

"How soon will your men be able to go?" Farnham then asked. "It's certain that Harold Mitchell will be going out to Nevada on the earliest train possible. And you'll need a lot of men to get on with them."

"You not worry about any of that," Ho Yang said. "You worry about getting elected to city council and I worry about all else. You already show me that you can only do me good if you get elected. You no good at getting men who can make people understand what power really is. You understand me?"

"Ho Yang, I don't need to be told I'm a fool," Farnham said bitterly. "This gunfighter hasn't made any of us look very good—including you."

"How he make me look bad?" Ho Yang asked. "I not have any part in it yet."

"That might be true," Farnham agreed. "But 'yet' is the key word. I want to see how your 'special men' stand up to him when the going gets tough."

Ho Yang stood up again. This time he fully intended to leave, for he had had all he could stomach of Farnham for one sitting.

"I going along myself," he announced. "I be sure things are done right. I go now to have men get word to Sacramento, where special fighters live. Then I go on train and into desert with them. When I come back with Golden Dragon, you be on city council and we both have wealth. Don't talk to any more business partners before I get back. Understand me?"

"I'll be waiting for you, without any new business partners," Farnham told Ho Yang through clenched teeth. "I'll be right here to see how you do. It's not going to be as easy as you think."

Ho Yang bowed slightly and left with a twisted grin across his face. Farnham watched the old man slide through the bamboo curtains and heard him talking to his wife before he left with Bard. As he listened, Farnham thought to himself how he would like more than ever to see Ho Yang have to face that gunfighter. Then he might just learn how hard it really was to see somebody like that facing you, somebody like no one you ever had to face before.

10

WONG LIN, the stout and intense leader of the Ta Kuos, sat alone in the darkness of a dim-lit back room, adjacent to an opium den. The Ta Kuo tong gang was in serious trouble. The gang was losing men faster than they could send them back to China for burial. And one man—a big gunfighter dressed in black—was entirely to blame.

The Ta Kuo leader thought about what he must do. His eyes, under their heavy black eyebrows stared abstractedly: his lips curled tightly inward above a thin wisp of goatee. The Ta Kuos had never lost so much in so short a time. He needed to put an end to the losses and bring his tong group back together in a hurry, or take the chance of losing the entire membership to fear.

Many of the gang members had mentioned to Wong Lin that they were going back to their spiritual roots for protection, turning to meditation and questions on how they might have angered the unseen powers. Their ancient religious teachings were beginning to call to them, even though most of the Ta Kuos had supposedly abandoned or forgotten them.

It was time, many of them thought, for rediscovery of the ancient laws. They sought help and strength in earnest. It seemed to them that the gunfighter was a dark spirit that had descended on them to decimate their numbers, for one reason or another, and they had no power against him.

Wong Lin, thinking in the dark, could not get the picture of the gunfighter out of his mind. This man had stepped in and had single-handedly stopped a well-planned attack against L. T. Farnham and his followers, an effort that would have broken the link of political support for the Ming Chins and thus ensured the Ta Kuos of supreme rule in Chinatown.

But the gunfighter had put an end to that dream—at least for the time being. And that wasn't the end of it.

Now Wong Lin had received word that the gunfighter had been in the tunnels below Chinatown and had killed even more of the Ta Kuos while making his way out with a woman and a Chinese porter who had once worked for Farnham.

As if the gunfighter hadn't done enough damage at the Palace Hotel. Now he had come into Chinatown and fired his pistols once again.

The Ming Chins had lost men against him as well, and in the same tunnels. It was said this porter knew some secret that he was going to lose his life over. But the gunfighter had taken him and the woman before they could be carried off out of the city.

No matter what the circumstances, Wong Lin realized all that had happened could cost him the Ta Kuo tong gang. He couldn't allow that to happen. He had to act fast.

His first challenge was to continue his quest to get rid of L. T. Farnham, and this gunfighter as well. It would serve the purpose of the Ta Kuos to get rid of Farnham, for then he would not be able to help their archrivals, the Ming Chins, in their political endeavors.

And as for the big gunfighter—he must die for his offenses against the Ta Kuos. There could be no other way now, for a great deal of honor was at stake.

Wong Lin thought of how quickly he must act. He must strike again at Farnham before the politician had a chance to bolster his defenses. Success would mean bringing the morale of the Ta Kuos up once again and possibly salvaging the gang altogether.

Wong Lin considered that he should act now, even before dawn broke. He could see a number of reasons why going after Farnham right away would offer the best chance for success, foremost of which was the fact that the big gunfighter had, not long before, broken into the main opium den run by the Ming Chins and had scattered their men throughout the tunnels and the streets of Chinatown.

Certainly the Ming Chins were now in as much disarray as the Ta Kuos. This would mean that the old leader, Ho Yang, and Farnham were without much protection.

Also, Farnham was likely in a state of extreme anger and frustration over the events of the night. Farnham was said to be a compulsive man under pressure—not one to watch things carefully. His two bodyguards were only as good as their leader, so they would surely be as vulnerable as Farnham.

Still, Wong Lin's main concern was Ho Yang. The shrewd old lord of the Ming Chins had lasted a very long time in a very rough profession, and not by being foolish. Wong Lin had no way of knowing if Ho Yang was with Farnham or not. But he did know that Farnham often spent late evening and early morning hours in the main Ming Chin opium den. That would be the place to strike.

Wong Lin now reasoned that it would make things much easier for his Ta Kuos if he could catch Farnham and Ho Yang together. If both men could be killed, that would give the Ta Kuos exclusive power right away.

While he thought, one of his men came in and announced that a couple of the Ta Kuo gang members had sneaked their way close to the doors of the brothel owned by Ho Yang. They were certain that Farnham was in there with Ho Yang, for an old woman had seen them and immediately two white men with guns had come out of the brothel to check.

Wong Lin knew the old woman was Ho Yang's wife. That possibly meant Ho Yang was there meeting with Farnham. Wong Lin knew instinctively now that the second raid against L. T. Farnham would have to get under way immediately.

Wong Lin moved quickly from his dark chamber with his man and into the main opium den. There he found two more of his fiercest gang members and sent the three of them to round up two more of the best fighters. He did not want to strike with a lot of men this time; the fewer the better for this purpose. They just had to be willing to risk all for the survival of the gang.

The five men, having sworn oaths of obedience, returned shortly to begin the raid. As he made his way through the alleys of Chinatown with his five men, Wong Lin felt a sense of intense satisfaction. He was going to make this sudden attack against L. T. Farnham work for him and he was going to have his tong gang come out of this stronger than ever. He knew it deep within. Then Chinatown would be totally his and Farnham wouldn't be alive to see the sun rise over San Francisco.

L. T. Farnham sat alone, brooding. It was dark and late and he wanted to kill somebody. Ho Yang had clipped him off at the knees right in front of his own men, and there hadn't been a thing he could do about it.

Now the two bodyguards were standing just outside the bamboo curtains, waiting for him. He had told them he was ready to leave, just shortly after Ho Yang had left. But he was thinking now, thinking that maybe he didn't want any part of Ho Yang or the Ming Chins any longer.

He didn't need any more tongue lashings like the one he had just experienced; and he didn't like the idea of having to split the ransom from the Golden Dragon on unequal terms. He had given way to Ho Yang's demand under duress, and he was stuck with the decision—unless he could find someone else with whom to share the expenses and the proceeds of going after the Dragon.

That would necessarily mean that he would be turning against Ho Yang and the Ming Chins. But as Ho Yang himself had stated, there were a lot of men lost now to that gunfighter and just a few more would mean the ruination of the entire gang.

He pondered the idea of approaching another tong gang. It would be very difficult at this juncture to pull it off. But anything was possible, especially if the gang thought they would have sole possession of Chinatown as a reward.

His thoughts were interrupted by Ho Yang's wife. The crumpled old lady shuffled past the two bodyguards and through the curtains.

"It time you go now," she told Farnham. "It very late. Very late. Ho Yang gone. Time for you to go, too."

Farnham was still stinging from Ho Yang's tongue-lashing. He was in no mood to have to listen to the haggard old woman now. He jerked himself from his seat and almost spat in her face as he yelled back at her.

"You don't tell me when to come and go from this place. You hear me?"

The old woman, well aware that Ho Yang dominated the politician completely, decided that she belonged up with her husband, over Farnham.

"You do as I say, or I tell Ho Yang," she snarled back.

Farnham boiled over and his vision momentarily blurred with rage. With a lunging step he brought his fist forward and down into the old woman's face, smashing the cheekbone and jaw on the left side. Her head jerked to one side and backward with the blow, and she spun a half-circle to the floor.

Farnham's bodyguards lunged through the bamboo curtains and one of them said, "What the hell! You kill her?"

"I hope so," Farnham said, his chest heaving, his arms shaking. "I don't have to listen to that from her."

"What about Ho Yang?" the other bodyguard asked. "What will he say?"

"Who cares what he says," Farnham retorted angrily. "I've had about enough of him, too. That's something we're going to talk about."

It was then that the doorjamb to the brothel splintered and six men poured through into the haze. The men were wearing red and Farnham yelled that the Ta Kuos were there. But it was too late.

Farnham's bodyguards both turned and pulled their pistols, but the invaders were already firing, knocking them back through the curtains and over Farnham, who stumbled to the floor.

When Farnham had climbed out from under the body of one of his men, he was on his knees, looking down the barrel of a big pistol.

"Mr. Farnham," Wong Lin said, holding the pistol in Farnham's face. "This time we do the job and that gunfighter not here to protect you." He brought the barrel closer to Farnham's forehead.

Farnham held up his hands. "No, wait! Don't kill me. We can make a deal."

"What you talk about, 'a deal'? Nothing I want from you."

"How about wealth . . . money?"

"Ha!" Ho Yang yelled. "You not have money with you. Besides, it not matter. I kill you."

Farnham pleaded louder. "Don't shoot! I mean it. I can make you rich."

One of Wong Lin's men encouraged him to pull the trigger, but Wong Lin momentarily waved him off.

"I want to know how you make me rich. Hurry and talk."

"I don't want to work with Ho Yang's tong gang any longer," Farnham said. He pointed to the unconscious old woman on the floor. "I got rid of her and I want to get rid of him. I want to join you instead and I want you to help me go after the Golden Dragon, in the desert. You know, the lost Golden Dragon."

"Golden Dragon?" Wong Lin turned to his men. They all knew of this artifact that had been stolen from the Chinese emperor and was worth a fortune.

Wong Lin turned back to Farnham. "You know where Golden Dragon is?"

"Yes," Farnham said quickly. "Yes, I do. Can we make a deal?"

Wong Lin's men were by now getting more and more eager to leave the brothel. If the Ming Chins somehow learned of what had happened and got organized, they could kill them all.

After talking briefly with his men, Wong Lin told Farnham to put his hands behind his back. One of the Ta Kuos then tied Farnham's wrists, while Farnham told Wong Lin the deal he had made with Ho Yang and the Ming Chins to work with them politically if they would split the ransom for the Golden Dragon with him.

"I could work with your gang just as easily," Farnham said. "In fact, I would much rather work with you. You are much younger and have better ideas."

"We talk about this," Wong Lin told Farnham. "But not here."

Farnham breathed a little easier as he was led up the stairs and out into the alley. He was blindfolded and led down a number of alleys. After a time, he knew he was on the waterfront, for he could hear the waves slapping the docks a short distance away.

"Did you move your headquarters?" Farnham asked Wong Lin. "I thought you weren't far from the Ming Chins."

"That not important," Wong Lin said. "Tell us more about Golden Dragon."

"Untie me and take the blindfold off," Farnham demanded, a note of fear evident in his tone. "If I'm going to support you, you can trust me."

"We wait a few minutes more," Wong Lin said. "Now, where is Golden Dragon?"

Farnham thought a moment. He realized he couldn't tell them where it was, for he didn't know himself. He just knew that it was hidden somewhere in the desert in Nevada Territory, and that there was an old Chinese mystic in Reno who had a map. And he knew if he told them that, they wouldn't care one way or another about him anymore.

"Why don't you let me lead you to it?" Farnham finally said. "I could take you out there."

"To desert?" Wong Lin said mockingly. "You take us out to desert? Can't believe you would go to desert."

"I'll do anything if we can strike a deal," Farnham pleaded. "I think we could be real good for each other. Once Ho Yang and the Ming Chins are done in, Chinatown could be yours. And I could support you from the main part of the city. Take the blindfold off now. Please.''

"Just wait," Wong Lin said. "How we know you tell truth? How we know that you can lead us to Golden Dragon?"

"I had a porter who overheard some of the Ming Chins talking about it at my mansion," Farnham said. "He's on his way out to the Nevada Territory on the train, to a little town in the desert."

"What little town?" Wong Lin demanded.

"It's called Creosote Pass. It's hard to find, but I can take you there."

"Is porter the Chinese man who gunfighter take from tunnels tonight, together with woman?"

"Yes. The gunfighter found the woman, who is the daughter of the man who pulled out on my business deal. I think we should catch the same train as they do and just follow them."

Wong Lin turned to his men and whispered commands that Farnham couldn't quite hear. It worried him even more and now he wished he hadn't said anything about his porter, Lee, who could possibly be going to try to find the old mystic.

Finally, Wong Lin turned back to him and he could hear some of the men who had come along now leaving hurriedly.

"What's going on?" Farnham asked.

Wong Lin pushed Farnham from the alley and closer to the dock. Farnham almost lost his balance, but stayed on his feet. When he had regained his balance, he felt the barrel of a pistol against the side of his head. Before he could yell or move, Wong Lin fired the pistol.

L. T. Farnham's brain exploded. His world flew out through the shattered skull on the other side of his head. His senses ceased to function; he grew limp with death, even before his body splashed into the water of the bay.

11

DESPITE HAVING HAD less than three hours' sleep, Lassiter was up early. He was eager to leave San Francisco and get the Mitchells and himself on the train toward Nevada Territory. He had a growing feeling within him that the trouble with the two tong gangs—especially the Ming Chins—was only just beginning, and that the worst of the trouble was yet to come.

Lassiter realized from long experience as a gunfighter that people in power who have been bested, and who are still alive to breathe hate, do not usually call it quits all that easily.

L. T. Farnham was of that persuasion, as were the leaders of the Ming Chins and the Ta Kuos, whoever they might be. Lassiter knew full well that running hot in their bloodstreams now was a hankering for revenge that would not likely stop at the San Francisco city limits.

Even so, leaving the bay area was of primary concern now. Lassiter suspected that L. T. Farnham and the tong gangs might strike again, and the last thing

Lassiter wanted to do was find himself defending the Mitchells, and now Lee as well, inside the Palace Hotel once again. He had killed or wounded a lot of tong gang members already, but they might come back in such force that battling them would be useless.

For that reason Lassiter had, the night before, suggested catching the earliest train out and relaxing only once they got clear of San Francisco. The idea had been met with immediate agreement by both Lanna and her father. Lee was certain that the faster they got away, the better their chances were of avoiding both of the two tong gangs.

Everyone was still very tired, but they were all as anxious as Lassiter to get going. Sleep would have to wait.

The sun hadn't been above the horizon much more than an hour when they crossed the bay to Oakland on a steamship and caught the Western Pacific, headed north and east. They ate breakfast and got some sleep while the train rolled on toward Sacramento.

Feeling somewhat better at Sacramento, they then boarded a long eastbound train of the Central Pacific, part of the transcontinental link, and waited for the engineer to set the engines churning for the High Sierras and across into Nevada Territory.

It was not going to be a comfortable trip. The cars were dreary and dusty, and the seats showed a lot of wear. Deposits of soot and cinder lined the window sills and filled every crack and crevice. Long stretches of desert country and the steep climb through the Sierra Nevada mountain range, which caused the engines to consume more wood, had made the inside of the train almost intolerable.

Harold Mitchell was disappointed that they could not have boarded the famed Pullman Hotel Express, which afforded the best of comforts to passengers. There were dining and sleeping and reading cars—all luxurious—which would have made the trip much more than bearable.

But the Pullman had left two days earlier and was, for the time being, running only once a week. Mitchell's party would have to be content with the accommodations available and do their best to tolerate the trip into Nevada Territory. They might be able to relax better at a hotel in Reno.

No sooner had Lassiter and the others seated themselves in the dirty train car than they were accosted by peddlers. Obviously these entrepreneurs sought to supply what comforts the Central Pacific lacked. The peddlers hawked everything from pillows and blankets to reading materials. Many sold fruits and vegetables picked fresh from the orchards and gardens of the Central Valley. Lassiter noted one boy—whom everyone was calling "Butch"—doing a brisk business in grapes, and was just about to call the boy to their seats when Lee nudged him.

"Ming Chins find us quickly," he said, pointing out the window to boarding passengers.

Both Lanna and her father noticed them as well, and their eyes opened wide with concern.

"How did they get up here?" Lanna asked Lassiter. "They weren't on the last train, were they?"

Lassiter shook his head. "No, they weren't. My guess is there's a contingent of the Ming Chins here in Sacramento. It looks like they're headed the same way we are, and no doubt we'll be getting a visit from them."

Lee nodded. "Many Ming Chins in Sacramento. Likely Ho Yang send messengers up here from down in San Francisco last night."

"Are we ever going to be rid of Farnham and those hatchet men?" Lanna asked.

Lassiter was thinking. He was looking at Lee, who had that knowing look in his eyes, that realization that he was as much a target now as anyone and that

Farnham and Ho Yang had decided the Ming Chins were going to find the Golden Dragon and get rid of everyone if they could.

"I don't think they intend to do us harm right now," Lassiter said, after some more thought. "If they were after us, they wouldn't have been so obvious."

"Maybe they're just getting bolder," Lanna suggested.

"Not getting bolder," Lee told her in disagreement. "Just getting smarter. They know Lassiter's guns. Don't want to lose more men. They will wait until they believe time is right to move. I think they believe I am going to lead you to Golden Dragon hidden in desert."

Lassiter nodded. "So they'll stick just close enough to keep us all guessing."

"If we get to Creosote Pass and don't look for any dragon," Harold Mitchell then said, "maybe they'll leave us alone entirely."

"It's possible," Lassiter said. "But highly unlikely."

The train pulled out of Sacramento and began chugging across the valley, passing miles of orchards and dairy farms, as well as large cattle ranches. All was vivid color and the bright sunshine bathed the day with a warm glow. But for Lassiter, there was no possibility that he was going to be able to enjoy the trip.

Three Ming Chins entered the car from the rear and began a slow and deliberate advance toward Lassiter and the other three. The porter said nothing to them, about where they had come from or why they were changing cars while the train was moving. He merely stared.

The three Ming Chins advanced farther. The one in the lead was old, with a lot of jewelry and a long, white beard.

"That one Ho Yang," Lee pointed out. "Very powerful man."

Bard, the big Ming Chin who had a score to settle with Lassiter, followed right behind him. The third man looked to be an experienced fighter in his own right. But as Lee quickly pointed out, they had not come to cause trouble.

"Ho Yang make the sign for talk, not fight," Lee told Lassiter. "They want you and me to sit with them."

Ho Yang and the other two took a seat about halfway into the car and waited to see what Lassiter might do.

"I'm going to take Lee with me and we'll talk to them," Lassiter told Lanna and her father. "Just wait here and don't go anywhere."

"I don't like this," Harold Mitchell said. "It could be a trick."

"Maybe not," Lassiter suggested. "It would seem that they aren't real sure of themselves. Otherwise they wouldn't bother to talk. They would just want to fight."

Lassiter got up and turned for the middle of the car. Lanna put a hand on his arm.

"Be careful," she said. "Please be careful."

Lassiter nodded. He turned once again toward the middle of the car, with Lee directly behind him.

"Just stay real close," Lassiter instructed Lee. "I know they might want to speak to you in Chinese, just to scare you, but don't converse with them. Let me do the talking with the old man."

Lee nodded. "I know you can do the job, Lassiter. If I them, I just shut up and listen."

Lassiter and Lee arrived at the seats where Ho Yang and the other two waited. The third Ming Chin was sitting in the seat opposite Ho Yang and Bard, and all three rose and bowed to both Lassiter and Lee.

When the greeting formalities were finished, Lassiter pointed to the Ming Chin standing by himself and spoke to Ho Yang.

"Make room for him in the seat with you two, then we'll sit down."

Bard showed his irritation at Lassiter's demand, but Ho Yang merely bowed and motioned for the third Ming Chin to move into the seat with them. It was obvious to Lassiter that the old man was a skilled negotiator and that he had hoped to have a man next to Lee, who might be able to get some kind of drop on him, or at least intimidated him.

After the third Ming Chin had crowded in with Ho Yang and Bard, Lassiter and Lee sat themselves down. Lassiter took the seat by the aisle, his hand ready to move for his gun if need be.

"We didn't come to do any shooting," Bard told Lassiter straight off. He opened his coat. "See, we ain't even packing guns."

Ho Yang looked sternly at Bard, and Bard stopped talking. Then Ho Yang turned to Lassiter, his hands crossed over his chest.

"He speak truth. We not come to shoot."

"I don't see any pistols," Lassiter said. "But I still see plenty of knives."

"We not give up knives," Ho Yang stated emphatically. "Knives part of us. Knives always stay with us."

"A knife in the hand of a man who knows how to use it can be just as deadly as a pistol," Lassiter pointed out. "Especially at close range."

"We never give up knives," Ho Yang repeated. "We come only to talk. Honor dictate that we not draw knives."

"Was it honor that brought you to the Palace Hotel to steal Lanna Mitchell from her room?" Lassiter challenged Ho Yang. "Or was that something besides honor?"

"In war, all fair," Ho Yang said, his arms tightening across his chest. "At times of talk, like now, only talk will take place. If war needed, then war will take place later."

Lassiter smiled slightly. It sounded like the same old condition presented by men of power: either you give in to what we want at the bargaining table, or we'll take it from you anyway, by force. But there was no need here to make Ho Yang think he had any power.

"What is it you have to say?" Lassiter said to Ho Yang. "We're wasting time here."

Ho Yang began diplomatically. "We have not met before, but I can see that you are a reasonable man. I have heard much about you and I do not wish to fight you. I want but one thing of you."

Lassiter watched Ho Yang without speaking. He could see Bard's eyes travel to Lee.

"All we desire is that man you've got with you." Ho Yang bowed his head slightly toward Lee. "Just him. Give him up to us and the trouble is over."

Lee's expression turne to one of fear. It was now certain in his mind that the Ming Chins believed he knew where the Golden Dragon was hidden and was leading Lassiter and the Mitchells right to it. But he quickly eased his tension, for he could hear Lassiter's calculated answer to Ho Yang.

"First of all," Lassiter told the old warlord, "even if I believed you'd leave the Mitchells alone, I wouldn't give Lee to you. He's with us and he stays with us."

Bard's face began to cloud and he broke in again. "Why not? What's he to you?"

"He's my friend," Lassiter said. "He stays with us."

Ho Yang glared at Bard once again. He said something to Bard in Chinese and Lee smiled.

Ho Yang turned back to Lassiter. "We do not understand. Lee is not relative. Why he so important to you?"

"I told you," Lassiter repeated, "he's my friend.

That's reason enough. You ought to know that, being you're a man of honor.''

Ho Yang's old face tried to hide the embarrassment. He shifted in his seat and recrossed his arms.

"You must know that this will mean great deal of trouble for you," he finally told Lassiter. "Lee must be very good friend to sacrifice your life and lives of other man and daughter for."

"He must be very important to you, also," Lassiter told Ho Yang. "For if you intend to make more trouble, you must realize that you will lose many more of your men, and possibly your own life as well."

Ho Yang grunted. He looked to Lee and back to Lassiter. "Why not let Lee speak for himself? Maybe he does not want to be responsible for all lives that will be lost."

"I not responsible," Lee spoke up, leaning over toward Ho Yang. *"You* responsible. *You* the greedy one who want Golden Dragon. You a tool to try and make me feel I to blame." Lee then laughed.

Ho Yang, for the first time during the entire discussion, showed intense anger. He knew Lee would never have spoken to him that way if the big gunfighter hadn't been with him. But there was nothing he could do about it. So he decided to try another tactic.

"Why you not let Harold Mitchell and daughter in on talk?" he asked Lassiter. "Maybe they do not want to die. Maybe they want to give Lee to us and save trouble."

"Harold Mitchell trusts me to talk for him," Lassiter told Ho Yang firmly. "He goes along with my decisions. And you've heard my decision on this matter. Lee stays with us. That's it; no changing my mind. Anything else you want to talk about?"

Bard then broke in again. Ho Yang did not stop him this time, for the old leader knew the time for diplomacy had passed.

"You can't expect to hold us off this time," Bard

said through clenched teeth. "We have brought in our finest fighters, members of an elite group. We'll take care of you in no time."

"Then why did you bother to talk first?" Lassiter challenged Bard and Ho Yang both. "Why didn't you and your special men just do me in right away and then have Lee and the Mitchells at your mercy? If you're all so invincible, why make this gesture?"

"We are men of honor," Ho Yang said once more. "We wished to give you fair warning. But now your time is up. No more warning."

"And your time is also up," Lassiter said to Ho Yang, rising to his feet. Lee got up with him. When Ho Yang and Bard and the other man did not rise, Lassiter added, "You had better think twice about ever wasting my time again. You come to talk and you don't have an open mind; you just deal out threats. Well, the next time you want to deal out threats, you'd better be ready to back them up. Understand?"

Lassiter leaned over to glare at Ho Yang. His strong stare made the old man recede ever so slightly, something he was not accustomed to doing. And Lassiter knew by the time he and Lee had turned around to walk up the aisle to rejoin the Mitchells that Ho Yang would certainly have told his group of chosen fighters that they were going to have their hands full.

12

LASSITER AND LEE went back to their seats with the Mitchells. Ho Yang, Bard and the third Ming Chin did not get up and leave right away, but remained there talking among themselves.

It didn't bother Lassiter that the Ming Chins were now going to get very serious in their approach to killing him. They had obviously tried to make it as easy as they could to find the Golden Dragon and had failed; now it was time for careful planning.

"What happened?" Harold Mitchell asked Lassiter immediately.

"It was what we figured," Lassiter replied. "They think Lee is leading us to the Golden Dragon. They wanted him. They said if they got him, they'd leave us alone. They got 'no' for an answer and now they're planning."

Lanna then turned to Lee. "None of us are ever going to desert you," she told him. "Certainly not after what you did for me, and how you helped Lassiter and me get out of those tunnels."

"I not worried about that," Lee said, turning to

Lassiter. "I worried about how to pay you back for saving me from shanghai. That what I worry about."

"I'd say we're even," Lassiter told him. "Getting out of those tunnels and then out of Chinatown would have been a lot harder without you. In fact, we probably wouldn't have made it. We'd have been trapped somewhere along the way."

Lee shook his head and I looked at Lassiter with sincere eyes. "No, we still not even. Maybe if you teach me to shoot guns like you, I can save you sometime. Then we even. I can't save you yet. I still a little sloppy."

Lassiter grinned. "Maybe we'll get some time and I'll work with you on your shooting," he told Lee. "But it takes lots of practice."

Lee groaned. "Ah, gun too heavy for *lots* of practice. Maybe I think of another way to save you sometime."

"Good," Lassiter said with a nod. "Why don't you keep watch for a while and I'll get some sleep. I want to be awake tonight in case those Ming Chins decide to come back and make trouble."

Lassiter situated himself for some rest as the train slowed down into Cape Horn. They would take on wood and water here, and once again farther ahead at Dutch Flats. There was also a scheduled meal stop at Dutch Flats. The cuisine at Sacramento had been quite good; but the lunch stop at Cisco had been less than tasty, the fare being stringy antelope steaks and dried potatoes.

Past the evening meal at Dutch Flats, the train would begin the long ascent through the Sierras, and the ride would be along steep grades and high cliffs. Despite the dropoffs, the mountains were scenic. Lassiter wished this segment of the trip would have taken place during the daylight hours instead of in the darkness.

But Lassiter realized his mission was not one of pleasure and the views would likely be disrupted most of the time anyway by his concern over the Ming Chins. That would not end until the tracks made their way into Nevada Territory and then out onto the desert.

Lassiter knew there would likely be an attempt by the Ming Chins to get Lee, and possibly Lanna, too. He wanted to be awake and alert whenever that might happen. But an abduction wouldn't be easy to pull off while the train was moving, and Lassiter concluded that they would have to carry out whatever plan they conceived during one of the stops along the line.

By getting good rest now, Lassiter felt he would be ready for the Ming Chins. And no matter how many Ming Chins there were or how good they were at fighting, they would have a lot of trouble pulling their plan off.

With this conviction in mind, Lassiter settled back into the seat for some rest. He was dozing comfortably when Lee nudged him awake.

"Something wrong up front," he told Lassiter. "Train still stopped. Should not take so long to get water."

Lassiter sat up in his seat and looked around. He hadn't realized he had been sleeping for the better part of an hour, way more than enough time for the train to take on water and wood and get going again.

There was no sign of the conductor, who should have been marching along the side of the train to be sure everyone was ready to leave on time. Many of the passengers were up from their seats and protesting, but the porter could only shrug. His job was to keep them inside so that there would be no further delays.

"I think I'd better go have a look and see what is going on," Lassiter told Harold Mitchell and Lanna. He turned to Lee and pulled the extra Colt from his belt. "Use this only if you have to."

Lee nodded and Lassiter made his way to the door of the passenger car. He told the porter he was going up to see what was holding up the train. The porter objected and Lassiter told him it didn't matter, he had to check out the trouble.

"Okay, sir, but if this train leaves before you're back," the porter warned him, "it sure as hell ain't my fault."

"I'll take that chance," Lassiter said, disembarking. He made his way along the train toward the front engine, noting how passengers along the way were all eager to roll once again. It crossed Lassiter's mind that possibly the Ming Chins had enacted some plan to hold the train up so they might try an attack against himself and the Mitchells. But that didn't seem likely, as the Ming Chins would have tried to get to them before now.

He noticed the two brakemen and the conductor just ahead, talking to one another and pointing in the direction of the engine. Lassiter advanced and the three men turned.

"What's going on up there?" Lassiter asked.

Both brakemen looked him over and the conductor asked him why he wasn't in his seat, awaiting departure.

"I'll answer that when you tell me why this train has been delayed," Lassiter said evenly. "I'm not a passenger who just does what he's told."

"I can see that," the conductor said. "You see, we have a serious problem here, and I don't want all the passengers alarmed."

"There's some Chinamen dressed in red up there, holding the train," one of the brakemen then told him. "They've got the engineer and fireman. Won't let them load wood or water. Can't say why, but they've got guns and knives. They don't want the train to leave."

"Did you say they're dressed in red?" Lassiter asked the brakeman.

"Red. Chinamen dressed in red. Some gang, I'd say."

The Ta Kuos. There was no question. Lassiter wondered how they had gotten aboard and why they were now interested in the ride to Nevada Territory. But he had no time to try to figure it out. The other brakeman had begun to speak.

"They didn't want to kill us," he was telling Lassiter. "One told us that he wanted us to wait a while, then we could take the train on over the mountains and into Nevada Territory. They want the train to keep moving, but not for a while yet."

Lassiter wondered what would make the Ta Kuos board in small numbers and hide out until they could hold up the train. He realized the answers could come later. What was important now was to get the train moving.

"You had best move somewhere under cover," Lassiter told the conductor and the two brakemen. "The only way we'll get this train moving is to free the engineer and fireman."

"You'll get yourself killed, mister," the conductor warned. "They mean business."

"That's a chance I'll have to take," Lassiter told him.

Lassiter moved on ahead toward the engine, slowly and with deliberation. As he neared the front of the train. His eye caught a flash in the engineer's cab as sunlight glinted off the steel barrel of a gun.

Ducking quickly, Lassiter moved back under the train just as the sound of gunfire erupted. He heard bullets zinging off rocks where he had been standing only moments before.

With a pistol in his right and his left hand free to maneuver himself, Lassiter edged along the cars, staying out of the line of fire. He moved himself completely under one of the cars to see what was taking place on the other side of the train. He could hear talking not far ahead, instructions being yelled in Chinese.

Lassiter eased across the tracks under the car. He

could see, as he peered out, that some of the Ta Kuos had taken position along the platform that surrounded the water tank, just back from the tracks near the engine. They were already aware of his advance and were preparing to stop him.

There was but one way to solve this, Lassiter thought, and that was to take them head-on. He would have to use the cars to his best advantage, but there was no other way. And every moment now was important to getting the train going once again.

When he got to the last car before the engine, Lassiter pulled himself up a ladder on the car opposite. Halfway up, he heard the sound of someone running along the top of the car ahead of him. He stopped on the ladder, cocked his pistol, and waited.

In but a moment, a head covered with a red cap and the barrel of a pistol emerged over the edge of the adjacent car. Lassiter fired and the head jerked back, the cap flying off. The pistol clattered down off the top and into the rails and ties beneath the train. One arm, with the tattoo of a dragon surrounded by Chinese symbols, hung limp over the edge of the car.

Now there were more Ta Kuos showing themselves along the railing of the water tank, just above him a short distance away. He was in the open now and they had come out to finish him if they could.

Before they could begin firing, Lassiter opened up with his big Colt and brought two of them down off the scaffold and into the dust beside the train. A third one fired wildly, then backed around behind the tank.

Lassiter knew he had to move fast toward the engine. There were no doubt more Ta Kuos still holding the engineer and the fireman hostage. And the longer they had them now—after losing three of their gang members—the more likely they would kill them.

Once atop the last car before the engine, Lassiter moved quickly. He watched the water tank and knelt on one knee when he saw the one remaining Ta Kuo move into view once again for a shot at him. Lassiter's Colt boomed again, spinning the gang member in a half-circle. He screamed something in a high voice and clutched at the railing of the water tank scaffold for a moment before falling off to the ground.

Lassiter reloaded. He tried to think of how he could advance on the engine and not put the lives of the engineer and fireman in more danger. He had just finished reloading when he heard one of the brakemen yelling at him from the top of the second car back.

"Riders! Coming this way!" He was pointing behind the train.

Lassiter saw a number of riders in the distance approaching the train. The volume of dust they kicked up indicated they were running their horses at full spead. In the afternoon sun Lassiter could see that they were dressed in red.

The Ta Kuos, in force, were on their way to the train. Lassiter knew there had to be some very important reason they would do this, and not just for revenge against him. The only thing that would be so important to them would have to be the Golden Dragon.

Lassiter knew there was little hope now of stopping the main group of Ta Kuos from boarding. The smaller group had held the train up just long enough to get the main force aboard.

The brakeman on the second car now pointed below to where the remaining Ta Kuos were running along the train toward the back cars. Lassiter could hear them just below him, talking in Chinese as they ran. There was no reason to pursue them; the important thing was to check on the engineer and the fireman.

Lassiter motioned for the brakeman to come up with him. The brakeman ran across the top of the second car to the first as gracefully as an antelope. His years of experience showed that he was as agile atop a train as most dancers were in a ballroom. He reached Lassiter and they scaled down the ladder to where the engineer and fireman were both standing with their hands on their heads.

"They're gone," the brakeman told them. "You'd better get this train fired up and going. There are more of them riding this way, and they'll be boarding."

The engineer looked past the brakeman to Lassiter. "Who the hell is he?"

"He's the one saved your neck," the brakeman said. "You never see anyone shoot like that before?"

The engineer shook Lassiter's hand. "We're obliged. You can hire on with his railroad as a troubleshooter anytime you need a job. Just tell them Ol' Hank knows you."

Then the fireman spoke up, trying to understand what was happening. "Them Chinese just jumped us. What the hell is going on here, anyway?"

"It's a long story," Lassiter replied. "Let me just say that there are two tong gangs from San Francisco at war and they've decided to carry it onto this train and into Nevada Territory."

"I saw them other Chinese dressed in black," the engineer said. "They've stayed to the back, in one of the last cars. Now you're saying they're going to fight these men in red?"

"That's what I'm saying," Lassiter replied with a nod. "If we can get all the people out of the last two cars, maybe we can isolate the two gangs back there."

"I don't want them running around on top of the cars," the brakeman said. "We've got enough trouble doing our job up there without a bunch of crazy gang fighters all over us."

"Don't go back to the caboose," the engineer ordered the brakeman. "Tell the conductor to bring all the passengers from the last two cars into the front ones."

"That's going to make them mad," the brakeman said.

"Tell them it's either that or be targets right in the

middle of a gang shootout," Lassiter told him. "You can't believe what these two gangs are capable of. Life to them is nothing more than a lantern that gets blown out when daylight comes."

"I'll tell the conductor," the brakeman said. "We'll hurry, so this train can get going. Maybe we can outrun them."

Lassiter looked out to where the dust cloud was growing ever closer. "Not likely," he said. "It's too late to stop them from boarding now."

"God A'mighty," the engineer said. "We don't stand a chance if all them riders get on this train."

"We'll just all have to do the best we can," Lassiter told him. "Push this train as hard as you can for the mountains and then hope I can somehow hold them at the back of the train until we get somewhere for help."

13

HO YANG STOOD WITH BARD and the other Ming Chins as the Ta Kuos rode their horses closer to the train. Ho Yang was as surprised as anyone, and he now realized it would complicate things beyond measure.

"Now we know why the train was held up, and why the shooting occurred at the front of the train," he said to Bard in Chinese. "This is not good. It will make us have to fight far ahead of how we had planned."

"But what are the Ta Kuos doing here?" asked Bard, also speaking in Chinese.

Ho Yang seemed to understand right away that Wong Lin had somehow learned about the Golden Dragon. He could see, even at that distance, that the Ta Kuo leader was dressed in a special, religiously decorated kimono that bore significance to his quest. He had called upon special powers to assist him.

It concerned Ho Yang greatly to witness the approach of the Ming Chins' most dangerous rivals in a greater number than he had ever seen them before. He was certain that their leader, Wong Lin, believed this to be the most important undertaking of his gang's existence and would fight until the end. There could be no other reason he would come this far with so many men and take the chance of trying to catch up with the train.

"They have a very important mission," Ho Yang told Bard. "The same as ours—they want the Golden Dragon."

"How did they come to know about it?" Bard then asked.

Ho Yang stood impassively, watching the approaching Ta Kuo horsemen. "Somehow they learned about the Golden Dragon from Farnham," he finally answered. "It can be no other way. Ming Chin would die before he spoke of the Golden Dragon. It could only be Farnham who told them."

"What do we do with Farnham then?" Bard asked. "If he told them about the Golden Dragon, he is no good to us any more."

"You are correct," Ho Yang said with a nod. "He is no good to anybody. When we return with the Golden Dragon, we will make sure he never tells anyone anything ever again—that is, if he is still alive."

"Yes," agreed Bard. "The Ta Kuos wanted him dead anyway. It was only that big gunfighter who saved him. Wong Lin has found him somehow."

Ho Yang now began to think about his wife and his main headquarters at the brothel. There was really only one place the Ta Kuos could have found Farnham and still have had enough time to catch the next train to Sacramento and to make the long ride to the train.

He remembered how his wife had interrupted the meeting he had been holding with Farnham before leaving to plan this mission and catch the train. She had mentioned at the time that there were men outside.

Now he realized that those men had to have been Ta Kuos. They must have then reported to Wong Lin about the meeting he was having with Farnham. Wong Lin must have managed to mount an attack later, while he had been organizing the operation to catch the train to Nevada Territory.

Ho Yang now realized that he would probably return to San Francisco and find he had been widowed. If Wong Lin and his men had found Farnham at the brothel, his wife would have still been there, and Wong Lin and his Ta Kuos would have had no use for an old woman.

"We must not concern ourselves with what has happened," Ho Yang said, taking a deep breath. "Nothing can change that. What is to come now is most important."

"We did not expect all this," Bard said in agreement. "How are we going to fight all of them?"

"We will find a way," the old leader said, holding his voice firm. "It can be done."

The car in which the Ming Chins were riding had but a few passengers besides themselves, all of them crowded up toward the front. They were separated from the gang only by a nervous porter who turned and watched them periodically, wishing he had been assigned to a different passenger car.

As Ho Yang continued to watch the Ta Kuos ride toward the train, a breakman came into the car and called the porter to the doorway. Ho Yang then watched while the passengers moved out in single file and were taken into cars up ahead. They hurried, their relief evident in their haste to get away from the feared gang members.

All the passengers in the next two cars back, as well as the members of the train crew in the caboose, also moved hurriedly to cars further ahead in the train. Soon there were no passengers or crew members left in the last two cars and caboose.

Ho Yang could only smile to himself; the big gunfighter was a smart man. It was plain to him that the gunfighter had enacted a plan of his own—to isolate the back cars and caboose of the train and pit the Ming Chins against the stronger Ta Kuo gang, which would soon be coming aboard.

It was a clever move and might work. With his men and the Ta Kuos as close together as but a few railroad cars, there would be certain trouble.

Ho Yang now realized he would have to use every bit of his tactical abilities to ensure the survival of himself and his special force unit. It would be very difficult to hold off the Ta Kuos if they chose to storm the car from the top and both doors. He would have to put men atop the car to ensure that the Ta Kuos had no easy way to surround them.

And he would also have to assign men near the doorway to the cars just ahead, where there were passengers. He didn't want the big gunfighter—or someone with a lot of nerve—trying to uncouple the cars and leave them in the distance.

Though it was much too late for reflection, Ho Yang wondered now if he shouldn't have proceeded on this quest for the Golden Dragon with more forethought. He had picked his best warriors, the fiercest and most highly trained fighters of his tong gang. They were few in number, but very strong. Against ordinary foes, there was no match. Getting the Golden Dragon would have been only a matter of time.

But there were no ordinary foes in this chase—least of all the big gunfighter dressed in black. Ho Yang had no idea how he fought at close quarters, hand-to-hand. There had never been anyone who had gotten close enough to challenge him without a weapon. This man had proved as formidable a foe as Ho Yang had ever encountered, on either side of the Pacific.

And now Wong Lin and his Ta Kuos had arrived in force. He had anticipated the gunfighter, but perhaps he should have considered that some other gang might also learn of the Golden Dragon, especially the Ta Kuos.

Bard was now rocking from foot to foot, watching as the Ta Kuos drew ever nearer.

"We'll have a time fighting all them at once," he told Ho Yang nervously. "We should have kept some of those passengers as hostages."

"The Ta Kuos do not care about passengers," Ho Yang pointed out. "They would shoot the passengers to get to us. Hostages would just slow us down. The gunfighter is trying to keep us back away from the other passengers, so that the fighting take place only back here. We will have to go on top of the cars and move about. We can't stay here where Ta Kuos would find us easy to kill."

"What about that gunfighter?" Bard asked Ho Yang. "He is something to worry about too."

"He is a great deal to worry about," Ho Yang agreed. "But he is in same position as us, now. He has to fight on two sides. And the Ta Kuos will want him as badly as we do."

Lassiter entered the passenger car where the Mitchells and Lee anxiously awaited his return. The passengers in the last three cars—other than the gang members—and the train crew in the caboose had all been moved forward. The front cars were now tightly packed, but it was better than being in the middle of a tong war.

Lassiter took some time to explain to Lee and the Mitchells what was taking place and that he was going to take volunteers and try to keep the Ta Kuos and Ming Chins isolated in the back of the train.

"If we can keep them at each other's throats the rest of the trip," he explained, "it will make things a lot easier for the rest of us."

"Maybe I must learn how to shoot this pistol better

now," Lee said solemnly. "It heavy, but I can handle it."

"It takes a lot of time to learn how to shoot one of those accurately," Lassiter told him. "There's neither the time nor the appropriate facilities here to allow you to get used to that pistol."

"But I tired of you saving me all time," Lee said with a scowl. "I want to go out and fight tongs with you. It my turn to at least help you."

"It would be best if you stayed up here with the Mitchells," Lassiter told him. "With the two gangs at each other's throats, they'll likely not be concerned about anything for the time being but knocking one another off. Keep the pistol handy, but use it only if you absolutely have to."

Harold Mitchell had been sitting silent, listening to it all and watching the approaching horsemen. He was wishing the train would get rolling so they wouldn't make it aboard. But he knew there was no chance of that now, not with the horsemen so close and riding so hard.

And he was now wondering if he shouldn't have taken Lanna's advice about giving up his idea to go and investigate Creosote Pass. He had his hands full at Glitter Creek as it was. Another successful financial venture would further ensure Lanna's future security—but that was only if they all lived to make the venture possible.

Mitchell realized he had committed himself now and decided it was important that he do his part to protect his daughter and Lee.

"Find me a gun as well," he told Lassiter. "I don't want to sit idly if those gangs break into this car."

"When I round up the volunteers," Lassiter told him, "I'll see if there isn't an extra revolver or two I can borrow."

Lassiter remembered from Glitter Creek that Lanna

was good with a rifle and could use a pistol as well. She now spoke up.

"I don't want to have to sit through this and just hope for the best," she told Lassiter. "Make certain I have a gun as well."

One of the brakemen then came to the door and gave Lassiter word that they had taken on enough water to get to Dutch Flats, where they would fill up for the haul up over the mountains. For now, they wanted to get started in hopes they could build up enough speed to at least make it very difficult for the Ta Kuos to climb aboard from their horses.

As the train pulled forward, pressing hard against the weight of the many passenger cars, Lassiter realized they would never get going fast enough to prevent the tong gang from boarding. And he didn't have a rifle with which to fire from the tops of the cars. That would have at least slowed them down some.

But doing that would also have made him an easy target for the Ming Chins, if one or more of them decided to come out on top and try to kill him. It was just as well to gather the volunteers as quickly as possible and formulate a plan to guard the forward passenger cars.

As the train gathered speed, Lassiter moved through the cars, talking to each crowd of passengers, putting together a volunteer force of men who wanted to help him defend against the two tong gangs. He got more men than he expected, and he got two extra pistols to take back to the Mitchells.

His force would be a pretty fair group of fighters in any situation. They were a mix of miners and frontiersmen headed into the mountain states, as well as a few gamblers and businessmen who had learned to use a gun.

All of them shared the knowledge that every little bit of assistance from each of them would make it that much safer for the passengers of the train as a whole.

If the tong gangs were allowed to carry their fight forward from the back cars, many passengers would certainly be killed in the crossfire.

Lassiter assigned the men positions within each of the cars. He also found a few who were willing to chance riding outside atop the moving train. They would be of great help to him when the gangs decided they would have to move forward to keep from killing themselves off completely.

With his volunteers in place, Lassiter returned to his seat with Lee and the Mitchells. Lanna and her father both took a pistol and held it in their laps, looking with fear out to where the Ta Kuos were starting to leap from their horses onto the train.

Lee was watching Wong Lin, their leader, very closely as he jumped from his horse and took position on a ladder partway up the side of a car.

Lanna asked Lee what the Ta Kuo leader was doing, as he was raising a small sword to the sky as he held himself out from the car and watched the last of his men board the train.

"He pledging his success or his life," Lee answered her solemnly. "He want Golden Dragon and to kill all Ming Chins, and Lassiter as well. Big trouble now."

14

WONG LIN WAS SURPRISED to have boarded the train with his men so easily. He had anticipated having to shoot his way on, knowing the gunfighter dressed in black was somewhere among the passengers watching. And he knew this dangerous man wasn't one who watched for very long.

Out of six men he had sent to board the train to stop it at this point, four had been killed by his guns. There was that much more reason now to put an end to his life.

He was also aware that the Ming Chins were aboard. The two remaining men had told him of their presence. Wong Lin had known already that they would have to be riding this particular train, as there was no other way they could follow Lee and the people the gunfighter worked for without catching the train with them. Otherwise they would have had to put a plan together to hold up the train, like he had, and ride like crazy men to catch up.

Wong Lin knew the Ming Chins would never have been able to pull a plan like this off. They just didn't know the country out here like he did. He was glad he had worked for the railroad at one time, and had discovered where all the train and stage stops were located. The change of horses had allowed him to lead his men to the slowed train. Without that knowledge, there could have been no plan.

Though he had at one time cursed every minute of his laboring years for the railroad, he now realized how well that investment of his life had paid off. He had known all along—and especially when he had gained power among the Ta Kuos—that he would get even for his hardship one fine day. And now his knowledge of the transcontinental railroad through the deserts of Nevada Territory was going to bring him to the Golden Dragon.

Another thing that surprised him upon boarding was that the last two cars, plus the caboose, appeared to be empty. There were no faces in the windows. Not one single person occupied any space on any of them. It made him wonder if the gunfighter and the others on this train were somehow preparing to cope with him and his men.

He knew, though, that foremost among his concerns at this time had to be the Ming Chins. They would have to be sought out and killed—to the last man—if they were not to be a problem once they reached the desert. This was the opportune time to get rid of their rivals and have nothing else but the gunfighter to stand between them and the Golden Dragon.

Everything had worked almost to perfection. Despite the fact that four more of his men had fallen to the guns of the gunfighter dressed in black, he and the rest of his gang had managed to board without more shooting. And they had managed to make it before darkness had set in.

The sun was falling fast now and taking over the train in the darkness would not be as easy as during daylight. But the hard part of catching up and gaining position was over. Wong Lin knew he had the strength of numbers on his side and that he would soon have full control of his future and his success.

Wong Lin was now gaining confidence with each passing moment. He was certain now that nothing could stop him from his quest. Gaining the Golden Dragon would mean wealth beyond compare and prestige both in Chinatown and in Canton, his native city in China. All people would speak his name with respect. He would go down in history as a brave and fortunate man.

As he and his men took over the caboose and last car of the train, Wong Lin discussed the plan they would use to gain control of the train. He knew they would be stopping again at Dutch Flats to take on water, and from there the trip up into the mountains would be slower. Once his men were in position, it would only be a matter of surrounding the Ming Chins and eliminating them.

As twilight fell, Wong Lin ordered his men to spread out along the tops of the cars and begin working their way to the front of the train. They were to proceed as fast as possible, yet to watch out for traps or situations where they could be killed. The Ming Chins certainly wouldn't go down without a terrific struggle.

Wong Lin would then learn by messenger where the Ming Chins had taken their stand and what the circumstances were with the gunfighter and those he was protecting. He had enough men to make his plan work quickly. It would not be an easy task, but Wong Lin was certain he would own the train soon into the mountains.

Ho Yang waited patiently with his Ming Chins, discussing with them the way in which they would lower the odds they were now facing against their rival tong gang. It was apparent to him that the Ta Kuos intended to take over the train as quickly as possible and surround them.

He could hear the Ta Kuos running along the tops of the cars already. Soon they would be taking positions in numbers along the entire length of the train. Ho Yang realized that before long Wong Lin would know where he and his men were located and would begin his plan to kill them.

He had an ally now, though. Darkness was setting in. The effects of being outnumbered could be reduced substantially when it was harder to see.

Ho Yang gathered his men and spoke to them calmly, but with strength.

"We must act fast, or die," he said in Chinese. "The Ta Kuos are moving all around us. Soon they will have us trapped. We must take positions along the tops of cars from where we are now, clear to the front of the train. We cannot let them gain any advantage."

"What about passengers?" one of the Ming Chins asked. "They will get in the way."

"Stay away from them if possible," Ho Yang replied. "Some of them might be able to fight, and it would only make it harder for us to stop Wong Lin and his men. Stay on the tops of the cars."

"What about that gunfighter?" Bard asked. "It is not likely that he will stay inside and merely hope for the best. He will be on top shooting."

"We have no choice but to take chances with him," Ho Yang replied. "We can move now and fight this man if we have to, or we can stay here in fear of him and die at the hands of the Ta Kuos."

The Ming Chins checked their weapons and prepared to make their way to the top of the cars to do battle with the Ta Kuos. Ho Yang would remain within the abandoned car with Bard—who would be no good running on top anyway—and two other Ming Chins who would defend him until death.

The train slowed once again and Ho Yang knew it

was to take on more wood and water. It was almost dark now and very soon they would begin their ascent of the mountains. If there was any chance for them to succeed against the large number of Ta Kuos, it would be along a winding, twisting mountain railway in the darkness. He sat back to wait.

The train was stopped at Dutch Flats to take on wood and water. Ordinarily, it would also have been a stop for an evening meal. But all the passengers now knew very well what was happening. The conductor had told the porters in each car to keep everyone aboard—or let them take their own chances at staying alive.

There was just a slim streak of scarlet light left in the western sky and Lassiter realized the darkness would work in his and the passengers' favor. But it wouldn't seem that way to the passengers; the night would make it hard to see and would only increase their sense of hearing. He was certain the coming night was going to bring a lot of hardship to all those aboard the train.

Already many of the women and children were weeping in fear, and the men were clutching guns and any other weapons they might have. Footsteps were already sounding along the tops of the cars and everyone knew both the brakemen had retreated to the very front with the engineer and the fireman.

"What will we do?" Harold Mitchell asked Lassiter. "We're sitting ducks if they all decide they want to come down into these cars."

"They're getting ready to fight one another now," Lassiter told him. "The last of their worries is passengers. They just want to eliminate one another for the time being. Then they'll worry about us."

"Oh, they already worried about you," Lee corrected him. "There no doubt they think you after them. That keep both gangs looking in all directions."

"Lassiter, you can't fight them by yourself," Lanna said. "That would be suicide."

"That's true, there's not a lot I can do against all them alone," Lassiter said with a nod. "But with the volunteers, we can at least keep them out of the cars and fighting one another on top."

While they were stopped at Dutch Flats, Lassiter took some of his volunteers and moved around outside the train to try to monitor the movements of the two tong gangs. But it was too dark to see much and he knew if they ventured away from the sides of the cars, they would have no cover and would be easy targets for the gang members.

Lassiter finally decided their purpose would be best served if he kept the volunteers inside. There they could defend the passengers better if any of the gang members decided for some reason to come down from the tops of the cars.

When all of the volunteers had taken position, the train finally pulled out of Dutch Flats. Lassiter remained at the engine, discussing the situation with the conductor and the two brakemen.

"I hope you know what this means," the conductor was saying. "If you want to keep the brakemen down off the tops of the cars, we're going to be in serious trouble."

"I guess you noticed, we've got the old cars on this run," one of the brakemen explained to Lassiter. "This is a small run and there ain't many cars together here, so they left us with the old ones—no air brakes. We've got to do it all by hand."

What Lassiter knew about trains you could slip into a thimble. But he did realize that with air brakes, the engineer could control the speed of the train. He could stop it whenever he wished. But with no air brakes, the only control for downhill speed was the hand brakes on the cars. And the brakes had to be controlled from the tops of the cars, by working each car individually.

Lassiter knew now that the fate of the entire train—tong gangs or not—lay in the hands of the brakemen.

The two men were responsible for keeping the momentum in check, ensuring that the train did not gather sufficient speed to derail or separate the cars. Yet they had to ensure that the train traveled fast enough to keep the wheels from sliding, which could cause a runaway that was unstoppable.

On the downslope grade of the pass—toward Nevada Territory—the engines would shut down and the train would coast. The brakemen would then have to be atop the cars to keep the brakes in check and to make certain the train didn't get rolling fast enough to derail and throw everyone down into the canyons of the Sierras—whether or not the tong gangs were up there fighting one another.

"If we get up over the pass and there's nobody to brake those cars," the brakeman continued to tell Lassiter, "we might as well kiss it good-bye. All of us."

Lassiter now understood fully that he had to find a way to get the tong gang members back into the last cars and keep them there. They would certainly not respect what the brakemen would have to do to keep the train intact, and losing those men would mean losing the entire train itself.

We've got more trouble on top of all that," the other brakeman said, pointing ahead. "Lightning storm. You get on top the train in one of those and you'll like as not get yourself singed."

Lassiter looked into the night sky where flashes of lightning were showing in the distance. Huge thunderheads were rolling down off the tops of the mountains, and soon the entire area would be a heavy field of static electricity.

"Those hatchet men will have the same problem," Lassiter pointed out to the brakeman.

"What I'm saying," the breakman told Lassiter, "is that no matter what, the two of us brakemen are going to have to get up there sooner or later and hold the train back. If I'm going to get shot by some Chinese gang member, I at least want to fall off a slow-moving train."

"You've got a point there," Lassiter agreed with a smile. "But maybe, just maybe, you won't have to fight anything but the lightning storm. With some luck, I'll push those hatchet men back far enough that you and your buddy can keep the train slowed down. Just don't come up on top until I've come back here to tell you."

"You haven't got a whole hell of a lot of time," the brakeman warned. "We'll be up to the pass before you know it. This train ain't that long and there's not as much to haul up the grade. You'd better do your fancy shootin' in a big hurry."

Over the puffing of the engine and the rumble of the train there came the sound of gunfire. The tong gangs had already begun their fighting. Lightning storm or not, Lassiter realized he was going to have to get atop the cars and start his own war against them right away. Either that or allow them to overrun the train.

As he started up the ladder of the first car behind the engine, Lassiter saw a bolt of lightning twist itself down out of the sky just a ways out from the train. A heavy crack of thunder followed and suddenly the sky was filled with jagged light, coming from every direction.

Lassiter realized he had to ignore the storm and concentrate on seeing the gang members. If he couldn't manage to push the fighting tongs back toward the last cars, the brakemen would have no chance of holding the train. Then no one would care about the storm or much of anything else.

15

As THE TRAIN BEGAN picking up speed for its ascent of the mountains, Lassiter checked both of his pistols and moved to the top of the first car. The storm continued to grow stronger and streaks of lightning were now common, popping dangerously close to the moving train.

The massive layer of thunderheads had closed the darkness in heavy and thick overhead. Lassiter knew he was going to have to work his way back little by little and try to push the fighting tongs farther back along the train as best he could.

He could already see them along the tops of the cars, like small humps that moved and shifted, as flashes of lightning exposed them. Though it was going to be dangerous on the tops of the cars in the storm, at least the lightning afforded some light to see them by.

But that would work both ways; and when the gang members saw him on top with them, they could come in stronger numbers than he could hold off.

Thunder rolled overhead, and the combination of

the rumbling from above and the steady puffing of the engine as it strained to pull the cars drowned out almost any other sound there might be on the cars. Thus if the gang members were moving anywhere close to him, he would not be able to hear them. He was going to have to rely solely on his eyesight and his instincts to survive.

Lassiter edged himself along the top of the car, looking closely to see where the gangs were fighting the most intense. It was hard to determine, as gunfire was now visible on top of almost every car of the train.

As the lightning grew worse, Lassiter saw men falling onto the rock slopes on either side of the train. He heard them yelling over the noise of the puffing engine, arms flailing as they lost their balance and twisted off into the darkness. They were getting ever higher into the mountains now and those who fell on the downhill side would likely not stop sliding for a long time.

Rain had now started to fall heavily as well, adding to the confusion. The lightning flashed all around, and the rain hammering against the steel cars increased the deafening roar.

As he neared the end of the second car back from the engine, Lassiter rose to his hands and knees to see better what was in front of him. A bolt of lightning showed the form of a man rising to his feet at the very front of the car just behind, holding a pistol out with both hands.

Lassiter moved sideways on the car as the muzzle of the gang member's pistol flashed flame into the night. A bullet smashed off the top of the car near his face. Sharp splinters of metal hot and quick singed his cheek. He moved again as another flash of fire spit once more from the gun's muzzle, and the bullet sang over his head.

Lassiter felt himself sliding and kicked out with a boot to catch the top of a ladder. The rain had made the car-tops slick and treacherous. Lassiter took a deep breath. His boot came to rest on the ladder. But he was still exposed to the gunfire, and he knew if he didn't stop the hatchet man who was shooting at him, there would likely be no need to worry about staying on the car.

Lassiter turned himself onto his side, his face twisted up into the rain. He braced himself hard against the ladder and raised his Colt toward the form now standing and taking careful aim. He thumbed two quick shots as another bullet rang against the top of the car just under his right arm.

The form on the top of the next car yelled and toppled forward and off the edge. Lassiter saw him plunge headfirst between the two cars, his body thumping back and forth from one car to the other.

Another form appeared to take the place of the first one, like some dark ghost drenched with water. Lassiter cocked his Colt once again but saved the round, as gunfire from behind the hatchet man suddenly caused him to arch his back and twist sideways from the train.

They were all around now, Lassiter knew, and the fight was carrying to the front of the train. It had reached him and he was right in the middle of it.

Lassiter pulled his second Colt and thumbed back the hammer. Two more tong gang members showed themselves on hands and knees. Both jerked with Lassiter's bullets and rolled from the train onto the rocky slopes on either side of the tracks.

Two more gang members appeared, and then a third. Lassiter managed to hit one of them, but the other two were ready to kill him when a bolt of lightning struck their car just behind them.

The shock killed both men instantly. One fell backward off the side, the other fell forward over a brake wheel and hung there until the jolting of the train moved his body into a slide down off the car.

Lassiter remained where he was and waited momentarily. The rain was coming ever harder and the train had moved ever higher into the mountains. When no one else appeared, he quickly moved down off the top and stepped carefully across to the ladder along the side of the next car back. He then caught his breath and waited before he started for the top.

Up ahead, he heard the blast of the engine's horn. He knew that was meant as a warning to him, for some kind of crossing or some other danger.

He turned and saw in the flashing light around him that the train was entering a long snowshed, a wooden length of tunnel constructed to keep avalanches off the rails in the winter. He quickly climbed partway down a ladder between cars. The sound of the train churning upward through the man-made wooden tunnel made his ears ring. But he knew there would be no gang members moving now for a while.

As the train passed through the snowshed, Lassiter took the time to reload and assess his chances of pushing the two hatchet gangs back toward the end of the train. He would have to do what he could to keep the two gangs at one another's throats constantly if he was to succeed. Getting the two gangs pushed together would keep them from concentrating on him to any degree.

Lassiter slowly but surely pushed the warring tongs farther back along the train. The gangs continued to fight violently, stopping only when the train entered yet another snowshed, avoiding Lassiter's guns as much as possible.

Though he had eliminated a number of both the Ming Chins and the Ta Kuos, Lassiter knew he could never hold them off if one or the other of the gangs decided to mount their forces against him. But they were fighting one another as well, and to concentrate on him would only leave them open to their rival's gunfire.

After the train left another snowshed, Lassiter made his move quickly. He had to work his plan soon, for the train was moving ever slower as it neared the summit. The slower speed helped Lassiter keep his balance better in the pouring rain, but it also helped the hatchet gangs.

He crossed the tops of two of the middle cars in succession, shooting a few gang members and driving others backward. He slowed down when he saw that the car he faced was alive with fighting hatchet men. He had reached the main part of the battle.

Lassiter lowered himself down a ladder to reload once again. He could see now that the car with all the fighting was the one with Lee and the Mitchells inside. In the light of flickering coal-oil lanterns, he recognized many of the passengers. They were crying and holding onto one another more than ever now.

A minister in the crowd had risen to his feet and was leading of the passengers in prayerful song. The words to "Nearer My God to Thee" came in a muffled chorus out to Lassiter while he got ready to again climb up atop the car.

At the top of the ladder Lassiter held himself firmly with his left hand, his Colt ready to fire from his right. He watched and waited as gang members now fought hand-to-hand just in front of him. They screamed insults and oaths in Chinese and stabbed at one another with knives, the bullets in their pistols having all been spent. He hoped those who triumphed would not have enough fight left in them to want to come after him.

As Lassiter watched, three gang members appeared from somewhere behind him. He emptied his pistol into them as bullets sang off the car all around him. Then he ducked as the train entered another snowshed.

Some of the fighting gang members were knocked from the train. He did not see any more until after the train had left the snowshed. Of those remaining, some turned and withdrew from the fight toward the rear. Others were trapped two cars down and began to fall victim to gunfire from two sides.

Lassiter now realized that the Ta Kuos had succeeded in surrounding the Ming Chins and were systematically eliminating them. He also realized that once they had finished killing off the Ming Chins, they would come for him.

Sudden movement just behind Lassiter then made him turn on the ladder. Outlined in a flash of lightning was a hatchet man in black, his hand raised. The arm came down in a strong arc and Lassiter reacted just in time.

His Colt now empty, Lassiter bought the barrel of the weapon up against the man's arm. The blow checked the thrust of the knife some, but not enough.

Lassiter felt the hot sting of the blade against his ribs as it sliced through his black leather vest and past his shirt. He had not struck the hatchet man's arm with his Colt, though, the blade would have found his chest.

Lassiter continued to slam his pistol into the Ming Chin's arm and shoulder. He could hear the man's grunts of pain. But despite the blows, the Ming Chin worked his way down the ladder at Lassiter, still trying to thrust the knife home. Lassiter knew if the Ming Chin got much closer, it would be difficult to strike him with the pistol.

The window to the car door shattered just behind Lassiter and a pistol emerged through the broken glass. The barrel went past Lassiter's stomach into the Ming Chin's ribs and there was a muffled explosion.

With a yell, the Ming Chin doubled over and fell down under the wheels of the moving train. Lassiter turned as a head popped out of the broken window. Through the din of the rolling train and the rain,

Lassiter heard Lee yelling, "I shoot good when I get close range."

"I'm obliged to you, Lee," Lassiter yelled back. He came the rest of the way down the ladder and stood looking into the car.

Lee opened the door and Lassiter walked in. The passengers stopped singing "Nearer My God to Thee" to stare at him. Lanna ran up from her seat and looked at his side.

"Lassiter! How badly are you hurt?"

"Just a knife scrape against my ribs," he told her. "It looks worse than it really is."

"You need help," she insisted.

"I'll wait until this is over," Lassiter told her. "The Ta Kuos have just about finished the Ming Chins. They're close to the back of the train. With any luck at all, I think I can get rid of them for good."

Lassiter felt the hot blood seeping from his side, but he was sure his life was in no danger—not like it would be if he didn't finish his task right away. If he didn't get back on top, no one's life would be safe.

"I'll be back again before long," Lassiter told Lanna. "Try and help these people if you can. Some of them look as if they're about to collapse from fright."

"Do you have to go back up on those cars?" Lanna asked him.

"I'm going to try to unhook the cars in the back from the rest of the train," Lassiter told her. "That's our only chance to keep them from coming back after us."

"I go with you," Lee offered.

"Stay here and be ready to shoot again if you have to," Lassiter told him. "It will only take one man to set those cars loose."

Lassiter reloaded both Colts and went out once again. The rain had lessened some and the train was almost to the summit. Donner Pass was only a few minutes away, he realized as he climbed atop the next car. As soon as they passed through another snowshed, he moved faster toward the back of the train.

His hopes of getting rid of the gangs arose when he saw that the fighting was now confined to the last three cars. As he reached the fourth car from the end, the train slowed down even more and Lassiter knew they were at Donner Pass.

With the speed of the train slowed down to just a little more than a fast trot for a man, Lassiter felt his chances of getting the cars unhitched were as good now as they ever would be. It would be hard pulling the pin and loosening the linkage, but that was the only way to get rid of the two gangs and ensure the safety of the passengers.

Ignoring the pain in his side, Lassiter lowered himself down the ladder to where the two cars were coupled together. The door of the third car from the end was open and flapping, and he could see both Ta Kuo and Ming Chin bodies scattered around the inside. He took a deep breath; the fighting was now taking place in the two cars further back.

Lassiter heard a voice just above him. He looked up and saw two forms in the night. One started climbing down the ladder.

"Move over and let me do that," one of the brakemen told him. "You'll lose your fingers for sure."

Lassiter relaxed and uncocked his Colt. He moved aside while the brakeman worked with the big steel pin holding the two cars together. Finally, the pin gave way just as the train reached the very top of Donner Pass.

The three cars and the caboose in the rear began to slow down. In the flashing light of the storm, Lassiter saw that the cars then came to a complete standstill. He knew that in moments they would be in a backward roll down the slope.

"That won't look good in the report," the brakeman

on top said. "But it beats losing the whole damn train and all our lives to a bunch of killers."

Lassiter could only hope that the fighting between the tong gangs in the last two cars was intense enough that they didn't notice being unhitched right away. He couldn't see anyone jumping off the cars yet and knew if they didn't get off quickly, they would all be at the bottom of a canyon before long.

"I'd better get back with the passengers," Lassiter told the two brakemen. "They'll be relieved to hear the tong gangs are no longer on the passenger list."

"You'd best get some medical help," the brakeman next to Lassiter said. "You're all blood. You get shot?"

"A small knife wound," Lassiter said.

"Small?" the brakeman exclaimed. "It don't look all that small to me. How you standing up?"

"I'll make it," Lassiter said, watching as lightning showed the cars behind beginning now to roll backward ever faster. "I've got all the time in the world to rest now."

"Thanks to you," the brakeman said, "we can all rest easy. I'll see to it the engineer puts you in for all the free train rides you want on this railroad. But whether you know it or not, we'd better get you sewed up. I'd hate to have to report that the man who saved the train didn't make the rest of the trip."

16

THE COMING OF THE STORM had been a bad omen to Ho Yang. Lightning and deep thunder was a sound that reminded him of death. He remembered that as a child during a thunderous night in Canton, in his homeland, a similar storm had changed his life. That was the night his father had fallen in battle.

This was such a night. As the battle with the Ta Kuos atop the cars came to a close, he knew full well that the end of his Ming Chins was at hand. And of himself as well.

The shadows cast by the coal-oil lamps in the car showed the faces of his men, each one knowing their end had come. As the Ta Kuos broke in, the Ming Chins fought valiantly. But they were quickly overwhelmed. Bard was knifed four times before he fell at Ho Yang's feet.

Now Ho Yang could do nothing but stand alone among the Ta Kuos and await the next moment. Their numbers had been too strong for his men to subdue, no matter their fighting ability, and now he himself was staring death in the face.

That face was represented by the Ta Kuo leader, Wong Lin, who moved forward through his men, a looming monster in the shadowy car, to finally stand in front of Ho Yang. In his eyes was a merciless glare that reached deep into the old man. For the first time in his long life, Ho Yang felt mortal fear.

"I have waited a very long time for this moment," Wong Lin told Ho Yang. "I knew that someday I would kill you and take you from power. I am grateful that it has happened sooner than I had thought."

Ho Yang knew there were no words he could devise that would hold his life much longer. There was no need to try. But if he was going to die, he would take his life himself in his own way. He valued his honor and would not give it away to anybody.

Ho Yang held his abdomen with both hands and looked hard at Wong Lin.

"I will make my own pathway into the next world."

Wong Lin sensed the old man's desire and stepped back from him.

"Take your own knife from its sheath and do it, if you wish," he told Ho Yang. "Far be it from me to disallow that which is rightfully yours."

Ho Yang pulled his knife and felt the blade. He filled his mind with the last words of his earthly life, reciting under his breath. When he was finished, he closed his eyes and opened his kimono in front, then placed the tip of the blade next to his abdomen.

Something within him tried to hold his hand—to prohibit the thrust—but Ho Yang fought the inner voice, believing that he must do this himself or see Wong Lin do it for him.

Despite the inner message to hold back, Ho Yang pushed the blade into himself. The air left his lungs and his face contorted in pain. He was fighting to hold himself upright, to die proudly, when suddenly the cars jolted and seemed to come almost to a standstill.

Through his pain Ho Yang saw Wong Lin turning to

his men and questioning what had happened, then peering through the window out into the darkness. Ho Yang put one hand against a passenger seat to steady himself, to keep from falling forward, when one of the Ta Kuos burst through the door and yelled to Wong Lin.

"The gunfighter has unhooked us from the train. We are starting to roll backward."

"Get everyone off!" Wong Lin yelled without hesitation. "Get all the men to jump, before we pick up speed."

But already the cars were rolling, gaining more and more momentum with each passing moment. The Ta Kuos began jumping from both sides of the cars in an effort to get off before it was too late. Wong Lin ran to the door of the car and looked out. Then, with a yell, he also jumped.

Ho Yang stood with a confused look on his face. Then the pain took hold once again, an overpowering pain that was filling every part of him. Against the inner voice, that which he had always listened to, he had plunged the knife into himself. Had he listened to his inner voice, he would still be holding the knife in his hand. Wong Lin had reacted immediately to the realization that the cars were rolling backward and had left him. Ho Yang now realized that he would still have a chance at life.

He might have injured himself in jumping off the train. Or possibly not; he would never know. As it was, he was bleeding badly and the railroad cars were going at a sharp rate of speed.

He made his way dizzily up the aisle toward the door, stumbling over the fallen bodies of his men, most of whom were dead. There were a few who were wounded and moaning in agony. One of them called out his name, and yet another took hold of his kimono. Another was rising to his feet, holding his middle. Maybe his Ming Chins might have survived, at least some of them. But now all he could think was that he shouldn't have pushed the knife into himself.

The cars were now moving at incredible speed, swaying and bouncing along the tracks. Ho Yang could no longer think, but wandered closer to the open, flapping door of the passenger car purely on what was left of his life force. The wounded men behind him became merely droning sounds inside his head, mixed with segments of his life that appeared before his eyes with incredible vividness and color.

He saw the pieces of his life moving before him, blocking all else out. He was not aware that the cars had reached a sharp curve and were now leaving the rails. Ho Yang was, in fact, totally unconscious and had fallen over when the cars had jumped the tracks and bounced end-over-end down into the bottom of the deep canyon.

The train had made good time after the two brakemen had helped Lassiter loosen the pin and leave the fighting tong gangs behind. They were well past Donner Pass and moving toward Truckee, where they would take on wood and water once again. From there it was on to Verdi, where there would be a meal waiting for the passengers. No one aboard could ever remember having been so hungry and so frightened, all in one night.

All the passengers were grateful to Lassiter for saving their lives and ensuring the rest of the trip would be without the threat of warring hatchet men. They were all aware of Lassiter's knife wound and were expressing their concern. No one aboard was of the medical profession, nor was there a nurse. There was but one person who could do him any good at this particular time.

Lassiter lay shirtless on his side in one of the seats. Lanna Mitchell wiped her brow and bent over him with a needle and a length of horsehair thread. Her father stood out of the way, telling concerned passengers that everything was in hand and that Lassiter was in no danger of dying.

Lee had volunteered his help and now held a coal-oil lamp for light. He had witnessed wounds being attended to before; but only by a doctor, and with the right medical tools. Nevertheless, he did not want to appear skeptical of Lanna's abilities.

Lanna was aware that the materials she had to work with were not of the best medical quality. But there had been nothing to use but the offerings of the needle and horsehair thread by a little girl who used them to sew buckskin doll dresses. It had been the little girl who had approached Lanna and suggested she make use of the needle and thread.

Lanna winced worse than Lassiter as she put the first stitch in his wound.

"I'm not very good at this," she told him. "I've never done anything like this before."

"Nothing different than a piece of cloth," Lassiter told her, gritting his teeth.

"No, this more messy than cloth," Lee corrected him. He noticed the look of disgust that Lanna gave him and shrugged. "It true: His skin nothing like cloth."

"Lee, will you hold the lantern still, please," Lanna told him. "Maybe if you just concentrated on *that . . .*"

Lee nodded. "Okay, I just hold light and watch. Not say any more."

Lanna continued to work as best she could, pulling the wound together and stitching it closed. Lassiter held himself firmly, keeping himself from flinching as the needle pierced his skin and the horsehair thread wound its way through each little hole.

It was not the time of day to be stitching a wound. Both Lanna and Lassiter knew that. But by morning, the wound would be so swollen that it would be very difficult to piece the edges together with any form of neatness that wouldn't leave a very bad scar.

And the ride down the mountains did not help, as the lumbering train jerked and swayed along the steep descent. But Lanna persisted in her work, and finally she made the last stitch and secured the thread in a knot.

"We'll wash that up when we get to soap and water," Lanna told Lassiter, trimming the end of the thread with a knife. "You're lucky. That hatchet man could have killed you."

"Along with many others," Lee added. "Lassiter have the strength of great Power with him."

"She's right, I was real lucky," Lassiter told Lee, sitting up in the seat and pulling his shirt and vest back on. "A lot of things could have happened up on top of those cars tonight. A lot of things did happen, but not to me."

Lanna then gave the needle and remaining thread back to the little girl, who was staring at Lassiter and smiling.

"If you need them again, tell me," she said. She turned and made her way back to her mother.

"I'd hate to think of needing another session like that," Lassiter said. He then turned to Lanna. "But if I had to go through it again, I would want you to be the one to do it."

"If I hadn't done it, someone else would have," Lanna said.

"Not as well, though," Lassiter told her.

"Well, maybe not," Lanna said with a smile. "But it isn't something I would want to have to do every day."

"No, it better to stick to cloth," Lee said. "Lot easier to sew, I think."

Lassiter smiled. "I would think there would be a lot of materials much easier to sew than my hide."

"Yes," Lee agreed. "Your hide as strong as any

hide I think I ever see. I think I glad you decide to come to San Francisco when you did. And I glad you still on train with us. I think hatchet men not ready yet to give up."

Wong Lin sat along the railroad track in the darkness and winced while one of his men fashioned a makeshift splint on his broken arm. His jump from the train had saved his life; but it had cost him the use of his left arm for some time to come.

They had been lucky, the Ta Kuos, in having gotten off the rolling cars before they had picked up enough speed to make jumping suicide. Staying on would have been suicide as well, for all the cars were now heaped in the bottom of a deep canyon.

But his arm hurt him and he was angry for the inconvenience. He was furious that the gunfighter had somehow managed once again to kill or wound more of his men and make things harder for him in his plan to obtain the Golden Dragon. Sure, he was that much closer by eliminating the Ming Chins; but with the gunfighter involved, it had cost him more than it would have otherwise.

And it had been the gunfighter who had seen to it that the cars were unpinned and left to roll downhill. It was this man who was responsible for his broken arm, and now for the delay in staying on the track of Lee, who was going straight for the Golden Dragon. This man in black was a curse, and he had to be dealt with, one way or another.

Wong Lin knew that he would meet this gunfighter again—there was no question of that. For if he had to, he would search to the ends of the earth. He would search forever until he found this man. And he would make him pay.

But Wong Lin now knew without question that this gunfighter was certainly not ordinary in any sense of the word. To get him and do away with him for good, this time he would have to have the best plan he had ever conceived.

But now, though, he would have to wait. He and his men would go back to the summit, to Donner Pass, where they would wait until some time the following day for the next train as it made its way over. It would be going slow enough that they could climb aboard. Then they would go down to Reno and continue their quest for the Golden Dragon.

17

RENO WAS TUCKED on the east side of the rising Sierras. As the gateway to booming gold and silver country, it was still growing faster than boards could be pounded together. The outskirts on all sides were tents and wagons—homes to drifters and wayfarers who were either getting set to make their way out to one of the many mines or were staying and becoming part of the booming local economy.

Lassiter and the Mitchells retired from the train in early morning to one of the finer hotels. Their intention was to sleep the entire day. But Lee could only rest a short while before becoming anxious over finding out what he could about the Golden Dragon.

At this point, he was considering cutting his ties with Lassiter and the Mitchells and going on his own. Lassiter and the Mitchells had no interest in pursuing the ancient Chinese artifact.

During the last of the train ride into Reno—after Lanna had sewed Lassiter's wound together—there had been considerable discussion about it. Harold Mitchell had had his fill of tong wars and crooked politicians. His sole aim now was to see what potential for development existed at Creosote Pass. He just wanted to forget about what had happened in San Francisco and on the journey across the Sierras.

But Lee's efforts were just beginning. Lee now believed he had a mission of his own in recovering the Golden Dragon and keeping it out of the wrong hands. He had seen considerable suffering in the streets and alleys of Chinatown and did not want either the Ta Kuos or the Ming Chins to gain more power for evil with riches gained from the artifact. He saw it now as his duty to protect his people as best he could and bring the Golden Dragon to its rightful owner.

He knocked on the door to Lassiter's room and waited until it opened.

"Lassiter, I need to talk to you," Lee said. "Bad."

"What's happened, Lee?" Lassiter asked, opening the door quickly. He closed the door and watched while Lee paced the floor and rubbed his hands together.

"Not what's already happened," Lee said. "What going to happen if we don't find Golden Dragon."

"Don't say 'we' when you talk about that dragon," Lassiter reminded him. "All that was discussed. The Mitchells have no interest in getting involved in all that. Don't you remember?"

"I remember," Lee replied with a quick nod. "But it very important. Maybe just a little help from you?"

Lassiter walked painfully to the window and looked out into the day. Though his knife wound had been washed thoroughly with soap and water, it still had retained some infection.

"I work for Harold Mitchell," Lassiter told Lee. "You know that. It's not that I don't want to help you, but I'm committed to Harold Mitchell."

"Finding Golden Dragon is very hard job for one man alone," Lee said.

"I know what you're up against," Lassiter said,

turning back from the window. "Maybe you shouldn't be getting into everything with this dragon so deep yourself."

Lee said nothing and Lassiter knew right away that maybe he shouldn't have spoken to him that way. Nothing he might say was going to change Lee's mind, anyway. There was a determination about this young man now that would keep him on his mission no matter what stood in his way.

"I know that you feel a personal commitment to finding that dragon," Lassiter then said. "And I hope you're successful. If Harold Mitchell gets his business done and you're still looking, maybe I can help you then."

Lee nodded. "I go now and let you sleep." He bowed and turned for the door.

Before Lassiter let him out, he told him, "You know if things were different . . . if I wasn't working for Harold Mitchell, you know I'd help you for as long as it took."

"I understand," Lee said. "Maybe I get lucky and find Golden Dragon right away. Then we all be happy."

When Lee was gone, Lassiter lay back down on top of the bed and stared at the ceiling for a long time. He fully understood that Lee could do a lot of good if he found the Golden Dragon and kept it from the tongs. And he was right in thinking it would be difficult and dangerous, especially going after it by himself. But as he had told Lee, there was nothing he could do to help until Harold Mitchell's business at Creosote Pass was completed.

Lassiter heard a knock at the door once again and rose to find Lanna in the hallway. He let her in and she sat down on the edge of the bed. She told him right away that she felt guilty about their leaving Lee to fend for himself.

"I told him I would help him once your father's

business was completed," Lassiter told her, sitting down next to her. "I don't know how long that will take, but it's the best we can do for him."

"What if something happens to him in the meantime?" Lanna wondered. "I wouldn't ever be able to forgive myself."

"You have to remember, he's taken on this Golden Dragon project of his own accord," Lassiter reminded her. "He's old enough to make his own decisions and live by them."

"But you know he's right," Lanna argued. "It doesn't matter that he's one person and there are no doubt going to be a lot against him. He's still right."

Lassiter nodded. "I realize that. It's been bothering me, believe me. But it isn't fair to put your father in a problem situation, either."

"Father can better stand it than Lee," Lanna pointed out. "There is no great rush to get to Creosote Pass. The place is hardly anything more than a few shacks now anyway. There's no hurry."

"That's something for you to argue about with your father," Lassiter said. "It's not my place. He hired me to follow his directions. Whatever he wants is fine with me."

There was a silence between them for a time while she looked into his eyes. Finally, she asked, "How did this all come about in the first place?"

"Life can deal some funny hands," Lassiter told her. "You never really know what the next card's going to be."

Lanna then bent down to look at his wound. "It's starting to look redder," she told him. "You had better find a doctor who can do something to stop the infection."

"I know I should get that taken care of right away," Lassiter agreed. "I intend to just as soon as I get some rest."

"I don't want anything happening to you, Lassiter," Lanna then told him.

Lassiter put his arms around her and their lips met. She did something to him, deep inside, something that brought her close to his thinking. He hadn't forgotten the fire she could bring to him, not since first meeting her at Glitter Creek. Since that time, there had always been a longing within him for her, to have her and be with her.

Their kiss was long and her response was as warm as it could possibly be. She then told him she knew what could take his mind off his injured side. She knew they had both wanted an opportunity like this since meeting again in San Francisco.

In Lanna's arms, Lassiter forgot the pain in his side—or at least it seemed to subside to almost nothing—while the sensations of loving her flowed through him like warm honey. Her touch brought a deep release from within and knowing her feelings for him made the moment that much more gratifying.

Lying together afterward, they both wondered how they were going to be able to help Lee and keep Lanna's father happy at the same time. The two situations didn't coincide at all and Harold Mitchell was deathly afraid of tong gangs now.

Lanna could understand that. It wasn't as if her father wanted nothing more to do with Lee. That wasn't the case at all. In fact, he had offered to find Lee some kind of job if he so desired. Either at Creosote Pass, if things worked out, or possibly in Glitter Creek. But Lee was tired of working for people.

So it remained that there would have to be something worked out so that Lee could be accommodated—at least for possibly one more day.

"I'll see if I can't get Father to allow you to help Lee for another day or two," Lanna said while she dressed and combed her hair. "That should be long enough for him to contact the laundry owner and learn where the Golden Dragon is. Father will certainly allow you to do that. Don't you think?"

Lassiter nodded. "I should think that would be simple enough," he said. But *simple* wasn't a word that had shown itself at all during this trip, and likely wouldn't.

"I'll talk to Father and see what I can do," Lanna said. "You get some rest and see a doctor. Then we'll be ready to get all this finished."

Lassiter walked her to the door and kissed her before she left. When she was gone, he laid back down on the bed and thought about sleep. It would come easier now, since she had been there and loved him. And it would be the first good rest he had gotten since the beginning of all this. He just wondered how things would be, and what would be waiting, when he awakened.

It was getting late in the evening when Lee returned. Lassiter and the Mitchells had just finished dinner and were sitting in lawn chairs outside the front of the hotel, watching hotel guests talk to a group of cowhands and discussing their trip into the desert to check on Creosote Pass.

Lee shuffled from one foot to the other, saying nothing, and Lassiter noted the forlorn look on his face.

"Did you learn anything about the dragon today?" he asked.

Lee finally broke loose. "Something very wrong," he said, the words tumbling out. "Old Chinese man no longer around. His laundry burn to ground."

Lassiter and Lanna both sat up in their chairs. "You found the laundry and it had burned?" Lassiter asked.

Lee nodded. "Six month ago it burn. Laundry man named Tun. But he not around any longer. No one know where he go. Don't know what to do."

"Are you sure there is no one around who knows where he might have gone?" Lanna then asked.

Lee shrugged. "Many say they don't know Tun very well when he was at laundry. Others say they never know him. He a mysterious man."

"Maybe there is really no Golden Dragon," Lanna ventured. "Maybe it's all just a good story."

Lee shook his head. "No, there is Golden Dragon. I know for certain that is true. This only make me know that I must find this man and learn where Golden Dragon is, before hatchet men get here and find him."

Lassiter noticed that Lee was watching him, waiting to see how he would respond. Lassiter realized it would be a lot easier for Lee to locate the old man—if he was still around—with his help.

He had told Lee during their discussion that morning that he couldn't help him find the Golden Dragon. But that was before Lanna had come to his room. Since then, Lanna had talked with her father and he had told her they could use some more information on Creosote Pass before beginning their journey. Harold Mitchell wanted to learn more about the town's location and how the planned spur line would run. He had agreed that while he and Lanna completed this task, Lassiter could help Lee for another day in his search.

Now Harold Mitchell was looking back and forth from Lee to Lassiter. Lanna saw her father's concern.

"Is this going to take more than a day to get settled?" he asked Lassiter.

"I don't know," Lassiter answered honestly. "It could take a day or two, or it could take forever. Who knows, maybe this man is no longer in this part of the country." Lassiter then turned to Lee. "Did you think of that?"

"I think of that," Lee said. "But there a baker woman I talk to whose eyes tell me she see Tun not long ago. She not speak very much to me. But her eyes tell me."

Lassiter turned again to Harold Mitchell, who was now looking out to where the guests had started petting the cowboys' horses. They were laughing and talking, and Lassiter knew in a minute one of the guests was going to beg a ride. But Harold Mitchell really didn't see them; he was too busy thinking hard.

Lanna then leaned forward in her chair and placed a hand on her father's shoulder. "Lee is responsible for saving my life," she told him. "Couldn't we give him as much as two days of help?"

Harold Mitchell nodded. "I guess so." The Golden Dragon had cost him a lot of time and money already; but he knew without being told that getting involved with L. T. Farnham had been his own fault and that Farnham's connection with the Ming Chins had started the whole business of the search for this lost gold artifact.

"We want to start for Creosote Pass by day after tomorrow, at the latest," Harold Mitchell told Lassiter. "Until then, you may help Lee in any way you can."

Lee's face beamed as Lassiter turned to him.

"Once we find that Chinese laundry owner, that will be enough to get you started in the right direction, won't it?"

Lee was ecstatic. "I know if you help, Mr. Lassiter, that all problems solved one way or another."

"There's only so much I can do," Lassiter told him. "I've had quite a bit of experience locating hard-to-find people. But I don't know much about Chinese customs and what to do about this Golden Dragon."

"I worry about that," Lee said. "If we find old man, I will then know what to do."

18

EARLY THE NEXT MORNING, Lassiter accompanied Lee to the ruins of an old building. It had once been the laundry run by the mysterious man named Tun. The building had been partially destroyed by fire, but the flames had been extinguished before the shops on either side were ignited.

"Why hasn't anyone torn this building down?" Lassiter asked Lee. "Why hasn't it been rebuilt and another business opened up? Did you find that out?"

"Didn't ask," Lee replied. "But can guess that bakery woman not want it torn down. She own building. I get most information from her. No one else seem to know anything about Tun. Or they don't want to talk to me."

"She's likely our only hope of finding anything out about him," Lassiter said. "Let's go see her."

Lassiter followed Lee to a small bakery across the street from the ruined laundry. There a middle-aged Chinese woman was kneading bread and serving customers. She was small and worked nervously, her fingers twitching about continuously. Her reaction upon seeing them was to become even more nervous.

When she had finished serving a customer, Lee approached her. She had already turned around to go back into the section of her shop where she did her baking.

Lee looked to Lassiter, who motioned to follow her back.

"Customer not allowed back here," she told them as they entered the back section. Her hands were covered with dough and flour and her small face was drawn into a scowl.

"There no other way to talk to you," Lee told her. "You make it very difficult."

"You should know, I don't want to talk," she replied. "This man you bring scare me."

Lee then began speaking Chinese and the woman looked back and forth from him to Lassiter. She nodded a few times, but then shook her head and went back to her work.

"She say she still not talk to us," Lee said. "She say we must go now."

Lassiter walked toward the woman slowly. He stopped when she turned toward him, her face showing fright.

"We don't intend to cause you any hardship," Lassiter assured her. "We only want some information about the laundry across the street, and the man who used to run it. Lee tells me you own the building and won't tear it down."

"Maybe it reopen someday," she said, working her bread.

"Then you must know where this man named Tun is," Lassiter said. "We have to find him as quickly as possible. It could be of great help to a lot of people."

The woman continued to work. "Don't know anything," she said, kneading her bread with her eyes down.

"It very important that we learn where he is," Lee told her. "Some very bad men—tong gangs from San Francisco—might be looking for him. We must warn him."

The woman now looked up at Lee. "What they want with Tun?"

"You know what they want," Lee said to her. "You know very well what tong gangs want from him, for he have map to where Golden Dragon hidden in desert. You know very well or you not be so secretive about where he at now. We must warn him about tong gangs, so you must speak to us."

"How I know you two not part of tong gang?" she asked.

"You know hatchet man when you see one," Lee told her. "And you know we not hatchet men. Otherwise, we torture you to get answers. Would we not?"

The look on the woman's face turned briefly to anger. "Yes, I know hatchet men," she said. "They kill my family when I a child and then my husband and children when I come to San Francisco. I know hatchet men only want to kill."

"I sorry to hear that," Lee then told her. "Hatchet men kill me if they find me. They know I do not want them to have Golden Dragon."

The woman studied Lassiter and Lee for a moment. "You certain you want to help Tun?" she finally asked Lee. "No one ever come before who know about Golden Dragon."

"We very certain that Tun must learn what is happening," Lee answered with a nod. "If you care about Tun, you will give us information. Then we can help him."

The woman quickly hurried over and locked the door to her bakery. She then put a "Closed" sign in the window and pulled the shades down.

"I want no one to hear me," she told Lassiter and

Lee. "No one. You must not tell anyone I speak to you."

"Just tell us what you know quickly," Lassiter said. "Then we'll be gone and you won't have to worry."

"Tun work on railroad and see Golden Dragon taken into desert," she began. "All men who know where it hidden but him have died. He only one alive. He alive only because he not want anything to do with Golden Dragon."

"Why did he leave here?" Lassiter asked her.

"Six month ago Tun get in fight with man about money man owe Tun for laundry," she answered. "They knock over lantern and laundry burn. Tun say that a sign to him that he not live where people fight for money any longer. He say he must live simple. So he leave for desert and never come back but for few times."

"Do you expect him to show up again soon?" Lassiter asked her.

She shrugged. "Don't know. Never know. He just come, but don't know when, if ever again."

Lassiter could see that the woman missed Tun and that the reason he would return occasionally was most likely just to see her. But her saying that he kept no regular schedule made Lassiter believe the only way Lee would get the information he needed would be to locate him in the desert.

"We have to find this man Tun as quickly as we can," Lassiter explained to her. "Do you have any idea at all where we might locate him?"

The woman looked hard at Lassiter and then over to Lee. The two spoke again in Chinese and she nodded. She thought a moment longer before she finally answered. There were few people she could trust, and those with whom she shared any kind of bond were now considered as close to friends of hers as she had. If Tun's life was in danger, then she would cooperate.

"He stay on edge of desert, in cave," she finally said. "North of town. He live out there now. Will always live out there now, he say to me."

"Why did he go out there to live?" Lee asked her.

"He want to learn what is the real truth in this life, is what he say," the woman replied. "He choose path to high knowledge. Must be alone for that, he say. So he go and not come back but for very few times."

"Have you ever been to the cave?" Lassiter asked her. "Would you know how to take us there?"

"Not been to cave," she answered. "But he draw me map in case I should go some time."

Lassiter waited with Lee while the woman shuffled to the back and returned with a scrap of paper. She laid it down on the counter in front of Lassiter and Lee, then used a shaking finger to point out landmarks.

"You can see where trail go off from main road," she explained, tracing a line on the paper. "It go back into where California at. He live in cave where California at. See, on map, where he mark that lot of rocks are and caves in rocks. Never come down again, but for a few times more, he said."

Lassiter asked her for another scrap of paper and redrew the map. It appeared that Tun had gone into the high foothills that ranged a ways out in a north-westerly direction from Reno. It was certainly solitary enough for a man who wanted to be alone.

"We thank you a lot for your help," Lassiter told the woman. "We certainly wouldn't have known where to begin without your directions."

Lee spoke to her in Chinese again and they both bowed to her before they left. Outside, Lassiter handed him the map and clapped him on the back.

"There, now you can finish your job."

"You not leave me yet, okay?" Lee said quickly. "It not tomorrow yet."

"There's no need to wait until tomorrow now,"

Lassiter pointed out. "You've got all the information you need to find this man. Go to it."

"Please, you help me find him," Lee pleaded. "Then you can go and be with Lanna and her father, and I not bother you any more. Ever."

"I don't see why you can't find tun yourself," Lassiter told him. "Especially with this map. It's pretty clear."

"I surely find him with you along," Lee said. "We can be back before tomorrow, when you must help Mr. Mitchell again. We can get horses and ride there fast. Then you come back and we both happy."

Lassiter took a deep breath and thought for a moment. It was true that Harold Mitchell wasn't concerned about what he did until the next day. After all Lee had done for him in San Francisco, the least he could do was spend the rest of the day helping him.

Lassiter finally nodded. "Okay, you've talked me into it. But if this map is wrong, or if we can't locate him by late this afternoon, we'll have to come back. Either that, or I can come back and you can continue searching."

"That a deal," Lee told Lassiter, shaking his hand. "That a good deal. I know we find him before you have to come back."

Lassiter wondered about his judgment all the way to the livery stable, where they secured two good horses and headed along the main trail that went north of town. It as not a main trail in the sense of those that headed east or west, or even south, for there was nothing but desert to draw travelers in that direction. That was obviously why Tun had selected the area for his privacy.

They rode the entire afternoon, while Lassiter's side throbbed with pain. On their left mountains rose into the sky, while on their right—to the east—was only a vast range of empty desert. There were deer and bighorn sheep grazing along the foothills above the trail, but out from where Lee and Lassiter were riding, no one could last very long without shelter and water.

The map proved to be very accurate. And for Lassiter—though he hadn't been in this part of the country before—there was no problem finding the section of rocks that rose jaggedly from the surrounding terrain. It was a massive framework of geology that stuck out from the surrounding country. The problem, he knew, would be in finding the hidden cave.

Lassiter took his time and looked the area over carefully, thinking where—if he were to seek such seclusion—he would select a cave that would be hidden, yet show the trails below and who traveled them. There were any number of caves scattered around, some close to the trail and some farther back and higher in the hills. Many of them could serve such a purpose.

After a time, Lassiter pointed to a section of rocks midway up the formation, a section where there was ample tree and shrub growth for firewood and good cover from eyes that might be looking up from below.

"There are quite a few caves up there," Lassiter pointed. "That's a well hidden part of the rocks. From there anyone could see who's down here and never need show himself."

Lee agreed and the two of them watered and then picketed their horses in a thick stand of mixed pine and juniper, where a spring seeped from a hillside and there was plenty of grass. After drinking from the spring and discussing how they would approach this man, they began their ascent of the ridge toward the secluded caves.

They climbed slowly and Lassiter watched carefully every step of the way. He had no idea what to expect from this Chinese laundry owner whose name was Tun and whose habits were mysterious. For all he knew, they could be open targets for an angry man.

They stopped to look closely at one area where

Lassiter's trained eye could detect use of some obscure trails. Lee then pointed up to a narrow opening in the rocks, an opening partially hidden by stunted juniper trees.

"I think that where he live. I feel him watching us."

Lassiter agreed. He had sensed eyes on them ever since they had dismounted from their horses and started the climb. The cave Lee had pointed out was a good choice.

When they had reached a trail on the same level as the cave, they stopped once more and Lee began to call out to the cave in Chinese. He yelled where they had come from and who had told them about the cave. Then he held up the map to show as proof.

It wasn't long before there was movement at the mouth of the cave. Soon a middle-aged man dressed in a flowing brown and white robe made from mountain sheep hides walked fully into view. Without hesitating, he motioned for them to come over to the cave's entrance.

Lassiter then realized how deeply this man must trust the bakery woman from Reno to show himself like that to a couple of strangers.

Lee and Lassiter both bowed and started forward. When they reached Tun, Lee spoke more Chinese.

Tun waited for a time after hearing what Lee had to say to him in Chinese. Then he spoke in English.

"I knew that one day the Golden Dragon would bring people to the desert to search for it," he said. "I didn't know it would be this soon. I only wish it had happened after my lifetime."

Tun was stocky and had a toughness about him that showed he had adapted nicely to life in a rocky cave. His narrow eyes were strong and dark and took in every bit of detail of everything he saw with one quick glance. He had taken on the instincts of the wild land he was living in, yet had retained the ability to talk to people whose lives had more luxuries.

He looked back and forth from Lee to Lassiter and formed a thin smile.

"You are two people who have not changed as fast as the times. Do you want something to eat?"

Lassiter blinked with surprise. They had just met this man for the first time, someone who had gone into isolation and didn't want to be around the problems of civilization. Yet he was accepting them as if they were long-lost friends.

The inside of the cave was far more homey than Lassiter had ever imagined a cave could be. There were animal skins everywhere to sit on, and a cool breeze, though not much more than a breath, came from the darkness behind to make the air comfortable. It was that darkness behind that made Lassiter ask Tun if he was ever worried about being forced out of his home.

"Only things that come from the darkness which you see are those things I bring myself," he told Lassiter. "There are many things back there, and they come and go when I sleep. But they are part of life and I accept them as they accept me."

Lassiter and Lee then learned that at twilight each evening Tun had to be out of the way of the entrance, as swarms of bats flew out for their nightly hunt.

"I know when they are ready to come," Tun said. "They tell me. Then I go out and sit on the ledge and wait until they are all gone. At dawn, they fly over my bed and go far back into cave. They never bother me."

"Have you learned what you came up to learn?" Lee asked him.

"One never learns all," Tun answered. "Only the little parts one is chosen to learn. So, what is it you wish to learn from me?"

Lee told him about the tong gangs and their search for the Golden Dragon, and his wish that the dragon not fall into their hands. While Lee was talking, Lassiter was looking around the cave and listening. Tun watched him a moment and spoke.

"You are a man who knows that secrets lie just beyond our reach," he said. "You might learn more about those secrets if you let me dress the wound in your side. Otherwise, you might not live to see these things."

Lassiter knew better than to ask the mystic how he knew he had a wound in his ribs. He just nodded and told Tun he would be happy to have him dress the infection. Lassiter had learned that help can come from many places in many ways, and that it was best to just accept it without question.

He sat still while Tun placed damp herbs on the wound and bound them with strips of animal skin. "Leave this on for three days," Tun told him. He then gave Lassiter a bag of different herbs with which to make tea, which was to be drunk before retiring in the evening.

Lassiter for his part saw he had accomplished all he could to help Lee in his quest.

"I've got to be getting back," he told Lee. "I wish you good luck from here."

Both Tun and Lee rose with him and they all bowed. Lassiter thanked Tun for his medical help, left the cave, and made his way down to the horses. He left Lee's horse and rode his back toward Reno.

As he rode along the main trail, Lassiter took one look back up to the cave. There were a lot of things to this life that a man couldn't see real easily. But when he did get a glimpse of a secret, it could be enough to change his entire perspective on life.

19

When Lassiter returned from the cave, he found Lanna and her father resting comfortably at the hotel. They were outside in an adjacent courtyard, watching a game of croquet being played by some other guests. They had both recovered considerably from the rigors of their journey over the Sierras and were eager to know how Lee and he had fared in their search for the mysterious laundry owner.

"We found him," Lassiter told them, "in a cave in the foothills south of here. Lee stayed out there with him. He should be able to move that dragon to a safe place now."

"Oh, I hope so," Lanna said. "It would make him feel so much more at peace."

Lassiter then told them about the herbal dressing Tun had applied to his wound and the tea he had sent back with him. They were intrigued by the fact that a man who hadn't known either Lassiter or Lee would be so generous. Lanna wondered if the man wasn't just overjoyed to see someone, and had offered his hospitality because he was lonely.

"No, that's not how it is," Lassiter said. "That man doesn't want visitors unless they have a real purpose in being there. He's something special, that man. I guess I can say I'm lucky I ran into him. My side already feels a lot better."

The talk then turned to the trip out to Creosote Pass. He and Lanna had learned all they could about the development in the desert—or all that anyone seemed to really know about what was taking place. It seemed the talk about the development had quieted some. But that didn't discourage Harold Mitchell. Come morning he wanted to get started.

"I believe it would be best if we began our trip even before it gets light," he said. "Some of the people here have told me that desert can be murder even by nine o'clock in the morning."

Lassiter could see that Harold Mitchell was every bit as anxious to get to his own dream of building up another town as Lee was to find the Golden Dragon and keep it from the tongs. Mitchell had learned that the planned railroad spur was to begin at a point yet to be determined between Reno and Hot Springs, then go north into the Nightingale Mountains. Creosote Pass, at the end of the line, was just getting started and would likely be a large town before too many years passed.

Though Mitchell had not been able to locate any of the main investors in the railroad project, he felt sure that he would meet somebody up at Creosote Pass, surveying plots for development, perhaps. Though Lassiter was glad that Harold Mitchell was happy, he suspected that somehow things weren't what they should be. It seemed odd that there weren't a number of people already working on the same idea of building the town and reaping the profits.

But that was up to Harold Mitchell. The man was paying him a far better wage than he could ever hope to expect from anyone else. If he wanted to ride out into the desert for whatever reason, he had a body-guard for as long as he wanted one.

As part of his job, Lassiter would be sure they had good horses and plenty of water and food to take with them. That was about all he could do, though his feeling that something wasn't right was active within him once again. Nothing would surprise him now. He had already learned that life as it seemed on the surface could make a fool of a man in a very short while.

Wong Lin and his surviving Ta Kuos left the train as it pulled into Reno. It was early morning and the town was just beginning to stir. Wong Lin hurried his men together; there was no time to lose.

His intention was to learn what he could about the laundry owner that L. T. Farnham had talked about the night before he fell into the bay with his head split open. Finding out what they could from the laundry man would make it easier to catch up to Lee. He would likely be with the gunfighter, and the man and his daughter who were headed for Creosote Pass.

Wong Lin was certain they had started for Creosote Pass already. But with any luck they would get some information from this laundry owner and then secure horses to take them into the desert. Creosote Pass certainly wasn't so large that they wouldn't find who they were looking for in just a matter of minutes after arriving.

Wong Lin and his Ta Kuos bought horses from a curious, yet respectful, livery operator who told them he knew of a Chinese laundry on the edge of town that had burned some time ago. But the building hadn't been torn down and maybe someone was thinking of reopening it.

In going through the burned out building and talking with nearby shop owners, Wong Lin found that Lee and the gunfighter had already been there ahead of him. They had asked a lot of questions about the laundry man who was now gone—a man named Tun.

"They wanted to know where he was now," one shop owner said. Then he pointed. "I don't know. But that Chinese woman who runs that bakery across the street knows him pretty well. That gunfighter and the small man went over there and spent a lot of time."

As soon as Wong Lin and his Ta Kuos entered the bakery, the woman tried to run into the back. She was quickly caught and brought back to the front, where she was held by two of the men. The fear she had first felt was now overshadowed by hatred.

"You leave my shop!" she hissed at them. "You no want bread. What you want here?"

Wong Lin ordered his men to let her go. They formed a circle around her so that she would not try to get away again, while Wong Lin told her in Chinese what they wanted.

"We learned you talked to people about the Golden Dragon. We want to know about the dragon as well."

Her eyes widened. "I talked with no one. And I will not talk to you about everything."

"People all around here saw a small Chinese man, a young man, and a big gunfighter dressed in black who came and went from here," Wong Lin said. "So you lie when you tell me that you have not talked to anyone about the Golden Dragon. Now, you tell us where it is."

"I do not know anything about a Golden Dragon," she said.

Wong Lin ordered one of his men to pull his knife.

"You will get your throat cut if you do not talk to me," Wong Lin threatened her.

"Kill me if you wish," she said bitterly. "But you will learn nothing from me." She stood rigid, waiting for the Ta Kuo to come forward and pull his knife across her throat.

Wong Lin thought a moment. It was obvious she

would face death rather than cooperate. He decided to try another means of getting information from her.

"Tell me about the gunfighter and the young man who visited you," Wong Lin said. "Were they nice? Did they tell you they want to steal the Golden Dragon from a sacred place? We have heard about this and have come to protect it."

"You have come to protect nothing," the woman said. "Do you take me for a fool? Kill me or leave my shop."

Wong Lin took a deep breath to quell his anger. He stepped toward the woman and looked down into her angry eyes.

"You say you will die before you tell us about the Golden Dragon," he said. "Maybe so. But you will die very slowly. Now what do you think?"

"You can kill me either way," she said. "Fast or slow. It is of no matter to me."

"Good," Wong Lin said. "Then it will be slow."

Lee rode back down into Reno to give the bakery lady a message from Tun. Tun was soon going to make one of his highly infrequent trips into Reno to see her, and learn from her at the same time if Lee was successful in relocating and burying the Golden Dragon.

Lee was anxious to get the message to her and get going toward the Nightingale Mountains, where the Golden Dragon had been placed in a secret cave. After discussing the situation with Tun at length, Lee had decided to bury the dragon and hopefully conceal its presence for a period of time—at least until the dragon could be safely returned to its rightful owner.

It had not been easy to gain Tun's trust. Lee had spent the night alone in Tun's cave, while Tun had gone out into the desert a ways to determine what he should do about the Golden Dragon. He had told Lee that he wasn't certain if he should reveal its location.

Tun had told Lee that by going out into the desert

and leaving him alone in the cave for the night, two things would happen: one was that Lee would have a lot of time to think about what he would be facing in going after the dragon, and whether he really wanted to. The other was that Tun would learn whether to put his faith in Lee.

Tun had decided long before that he would never again touch the Golden Dragon. He felt, as the only Chinese railroad worker who had been left alive after its placement in the cave, that he alone should know of its whereabouts. But Lee's determined effort to keep the Golden Dragon from harm had made Tun wonder if he should reconsider his position.

Lee had worried that Tun might need more than a night in the desert to make up his mind. But Tun had returned sooner than expected. And he had made his mind up fully.

Lee had been awakened by the rushing sound of the bats returning to the cave. He had lain with his eyes open while a long, squeaking cloud of black had rushed over him. Tun had entered the cave behind the flow of bats with a smile on his face, willing to tell him where the Golden Dragon was.

Tun had decided that Lee was sincere and that he could find a location to bury the dragon before any harm came to it. He knew Lee had spent the night alone in the cave and had experienced many fears, and had dealt with them satisfactorily. If anyone but himself was ever to touch the Golden Dragon, it was this man, Lee.

"You will find a small trail that leads to the west of the main trail to Creosote Pass," Tun had told Lee. "You must travel just two miles to where there are underground caverns. You will see a lone hill with only two trees on it. If you sit under the biggest tree and wait until an hour before sunset, the sun will shine at just the right angle on a blue stone that marks the entrance to where the Golden Dragon rests. Good luck, my friend.

Thus it was with great eagerness to get into the Nightingale Mountains and find the Golden Dragon that Lee tied his horse in front of the bakery and hurried inside. The Chinese woman was startled by his appearance, as was Wong Lin and the rest of his Ta Kuos.

Lee turned to run but was grabbed by one of the Ta Kuos. He was then brought over to stand with the woman. Fear crept into him as he realized that Wong Lin and his Ta Kuos would do anything to get information about the Golden Dragon.

But not only was Lee frightened, he was downright surprised. He had thought it would have taken longer for any surviving tong gang members to get to Reno. He could see that Wong Lin had injured his arm and was wearing a sling, but that his drive to find the Golden Dragon was pushing him past physical pain.

"So, we are more lucky than we thought," said Wong Lin, smiling broadly and speaking in Chinese to Lee. "We have found you. Where is the big gunfighter? We want him too."

"He will be coming soon," Lee said quickly, hoping to make Wong Lin afraid. "You had better let this woman and myself go. The big gunfighter will kill all of you."

Wong Lin snorted. "The big gunfighter did not come with you, so the big gunfighter will not come later, either. This is what I think. Is that not so?"

"He will come," Lee promised.

"We will not be here when he comes, though," Wong Lin said dryly. "I wish we could be, for I would like to see him die. But we will be gone. You are going to take us to the Golden Dragon."

Lee's face clouded with anger. "I will not take you anywhere."

"I think you will," Wong Lin said between pursed

lips. He motioned to one of his men, who grabbed the woman and put a knife to her throat.

"Let her go!" Lee said, rushing forward. He was stopped and held by three of the Ta Kuos.

"Would you like to see how she bleeds?" Wong Lin asked Lee. "Or would you rather take us to the Golden Dragon?"

"Do not take them!" the woman said quickly. "Do nothing for them. I would rather die than have them know where the Golden Dragon is."

"Ah, then you wish to die in front of this young man?" Wong Lin asked her. "He does not wish you to die."

"I do not care what he wishes," she hissed. "Kill me!"

Wong Lin turned to Lee. "It is something she wishes."

Lee's eyes widened. He realized they would kill her and not even care about it. He didn't want to see the woman killed, and if she was, Tun would certainly never forgive him. He had to tell them something.

"Wait!" he yelled to Wong Lin. "You let her go and I will take you to the Golden Dragon. But you must let her go."

A sneer crossed Wong Lin's face and he stepped toward Lee.

"How do we know that if we let her go, you will take us to the Golden Dragon? Maybe she also knows where it is. Maybe we will take her as well."

"She does not know where the Golden Dragon is," Lee informed them bluntly. "Only I do. And I know it is in cave north of here, just off of road to Creosote Pass. But you will never find it without me. There is a secret."

"Ha!" Wong Lin yelled. "There is no secret."

"Kill me, then," Lee challenged. "See if you find the Golden Dragon."

Wong Lin looked to his men. Finally, he turned

back to Lee and nodded. "We will let the woman go and you will show us where the Golden Dragon is. Otherwise, we will kill you and come back and kill the woman. Understand?"

"I have no choice, it seems," Lee said.

"That is true," Wong Lin said, the sneer still on his face. "You have no choice."

20

"I CAME ALL THE WAY out here to learn *this?*"

Harold Mitchell fumed, pacing the creaky board-walk in front of a run-down building on the edge of Creosote Pass. It had served, for a very short time, as a temporary depot during the planning stages of the spur line. But now it was abandoned; there would be no spur line.

A few minutes before, a bartender in a small log saloon had informed them that the plans to bring a spur up from the main line had been canceled. That was the word brought just the day before by a number of men who had planned to work on the rails. The two men who had been manning the temporary depot had left that morning. Creosote Pass would remain nothing more than a dusty stop in the desert.

"I just can't believe this has happened," Harold Mitchell continued.

"It's your own fault, Father," Lanna said with irritation. "I told you this was a crazy idea. Look what we've gone through, and for what?"

"Lanna, if you don't take chances, you never get anywhere."

"There are some chances that get people killed, Father," Lanna argued.

Harold Mitchell stared at his daughter a moment and turned to kick dirt from the street in front of the abandoned depot. Lanna was still angry and Lassiter took her arm gently and turned her to him.

"Don't be so hard on him. There was no way of knowing this would happen. Everyone in Reno thought the plan was still on."

"Whose side are you on now?" Lanna asked him.

"I'm not taking sides," Lassiter replied. "But it won't do any good to argue about it now."

"I just don't want to stay in this desert rathole another minute," Lanna said. She turned to her father. "Let's get back up to Glitter Creek, where we belong."

Harold Mitchell had to agree with his daughter on this point. He took one last look over the town, frowning with disgust, and started down for the saloon where the horses were tied.

Lassiter followed a short way behind with Lanna. She continued to vent her feelings over coming all the way out from San Francisco into a vast and deserted stretch of scrub brush and parched soil, only to learn it had all been a complete waste of time and money.

But they were all alive, Lassiter thought to himself. And thanks to Tun his rib wound was nearly healed. He tried again to calm Lanna down.

"Just think of it as being all over now," he told her. "Everyone is alive and safe, and all we have to do is get back down to Reno, and you and your father can head back to Glitter Creek. Think of the stories you can tell your friends up there."

"Stories no one who hadn't been there would believe," Lanna said. "But you're right; there's no use in harassing Father about it now. Chances are, if he had it to do over again, nothing would change any-way.''

Lassiter smiled. Lanna knew her father pretty well. And she knew she wasn't going to change him. A man like Harold Mitchell valued his entire existence on the excitement of building something where there had never been anything before. Lassiter's own theory was that maybe things should be left alone in most cases. But Harold Mitchell had a good heart and what he wanted to do was his own business.

Lassiter took a long last look at Creosote Pass as they reached the horses. They filled their canteens with water once again and began the ride back. Evening was approaching, and the desert was cooling down. The moon would be full too. Thus, riding back to Reno in the dark was a far better prospect than facing it in the heat of the day.

But an hour out of Creosote Pass, Lassiter saw dust rising in the distance. Riders were coming at a fast pace. They were in a hurry on the desert: that meant they wanted to get someplace before nightfall.

There was still a good three hours of daylight left and the rising dust formed a hazy cloud as it hung in the air above the trail. Lassiter looked for a suitable place from which to observe the riders. Finally, he pointed to a location a short ways ahead.

"Let's move onto that hill off the trail," Lassiter told Lanna and her father. "We'll see who it is before we meet them."

Lassiter led them off the trail, along a hill covered with brush and crusted white soil. It would afford a good place from which to look out across the harsh country at the dust cloud that was moving steadily closer.

It took little time before Lassiter could see that the main body of oncoming riders was dressed in red. At least some of the Ta Kuos had managed to get themselves off the rolling cars and find their way up into the desert.

Lassiter wondered how they had managed to find their way out into the desert. The riders were now close enough that he could see that the man leading them had his left arm in a sling, and that a smaller man was riding right beside him.

"Isn't that Lee?" Lanna asked, recognizing his clothing.

"It is," Lassiter answered. They must have found him somehow and are forcing him into showing them where the Golden Dragon is hidden."

"We've got to help him," Lanna said. "But what are we going to do?"

"We'll just have to take Lee away from them," Lassiter said. "There's no other way."

"What do you propose to do?" Harold Mitchell asked. "You can't just ride up and demand they give Lee up to you."

"That's not what I had in mind," Lassiter said, watching the riders draw nearer. "If we get with the sun at our backs and go straight at them, my guess is they'll scatter with hardly a fight."

"Won't that be putting Lee's life in danger?" Lanna asked. "Won't they kill him?"

"Shooting Lee would be a fool thing for them to do," Lassiter pointed out. "They won't do that, not if they want to learn where that dragon is buried. Lee would be dead already if they had no more use for him. And after he takes them to the dragon, they'll kill him for sure. So he has nothing to lose."

"It looks like there's a lot of them, Lassiter," Harold Mitchell said.

"There's a lot fewer of them now than the other night on the top of that train," Lassiter reminded him. "And there's a lot more room out here. Let's go while we've still got the chance to set up and surprise them."

Lassiter led them down off the hill and across the

trail to a position where there was more brush to hide them. Lanna took the extra pistol Lassiter had been carrying and Harold Mitchell checked the Colt he had been given to use on the train.

"Don't worry about hitting any of them," Lassiter said. "If we just spray them with lead for a while, they'll head for cover."

"I'm not used to this kind of thing," Harold Mitchell said. "But since Lee has been so good to Lanna, I'll consider myself a brush fighter for the time being."

Lanna then took a deep breath herself. "I much prefer shooting a rifle," she said, holding up the Colt. "I know I can't hit anything with this."

"If we had a rifle, I'd give it to you," Lassiter said. "Just stay low over your horse and go straight for them. With the sun behind us, they won't take the time to get into position to fight us. We just need to surprise them and get Lee away safely."

Lassiter positioned them for the charge from the brush. The three would come from a scattered formation, riding evenly, shooting as fast as they could. Lassiter hoped that the surprise would overwhelm the Ta Kuos and they would have to retreat without putting up much of a fight.

Lee and the Ta Kuos rode around a group of low hills, coming ever closer. Lassiter noted there was less than a dozen of Wong Lin's men left now; a lot better odds than he had ever enjoyed before against them. He waited until they had ridden to just the right place along the trail, where the falling sun would blind them against the attack. After but a few moments of waiting, he knew the time was right.

Lassiter then yelled and spurred his horse into a dead run, with Lanna and her father coming out from the brush at the same time. Lassiter rode hard toward the leader, Wong Lin, and fired. But Wong Lin had suddenly reined in his horse and a Ta Kuo just next to him rode into the bullet and fell from his saddle.

Lassiter continued to ride straight at Wong Lin, who shouted oaths at him in Chinese. Wong Lin, able to ride only with his good hand and unable to shoot at all, could only stay behind his men, who desperately tried to build a front against Lassiter's guns.

Two of Wong Lin's men spurred their horses toward Lassiter, but were falling from their saddles before they had even gotten shots off at him. With Lanna and her father both shooting as well, the Ta Kuos were soon a mass of confusion, trying to control their startled horses.

Wong Lin was concentrating on Lassiter and did not see Lanna riding toward him until it was too late. A flame burst from the barrel of her Colt and he felt the hot pain of a bullet searing across the top of his left shoulder. Had the wound been in his right shoulder, he would have been forced to drop the reins and wouldn't have been able to stay on his horse.

Screaming even more oaths, Wong Lin led his men in retreat. Another one of them had fallen to a shot from Harold Mitchell's Colt and Lanna had managed to wound yet another.

While the Ta Kuos retreated together up along the hills, Lee rode toward Lassiter, kicking the horse as hard as he could. He pulled to a stop in front of Lassiter's horse as Lanna and her father joined them.

"You always at right place at right time," Lee told Lassiter. "Lucky for us." Then he looked at Lanna. "How you learn to shoot like that? Pretty good."

"You saved my life," Lanna told Lee. "The least I can do is try to help you."

Lee bowed. "Maybe some day you good as Lassiter," he said with a grin. "But take lots of practice."

"How did they find you?" Lassiter asked him.

"I go to bakery to give woman a message from Tun.

They were already there. I tell you more when we get to where Golden Dragon is hidden.''

"It would be best if we got there as quickly as possible," Lassiter said. "I have a feeling the Ta Kuos won't wait all that long before they come after us."

Wong Lin allowed one of his men to tie a strip of cloth to his bleeding shoulder. Once again he had been beaten by the big gunfighter, and he couldn't contain his anger.

"We are so close to the Golden Dragon and he comes again," Wong Lin was saying. "But we will not be stopped. We will not!"

"Maybe this gunfighter is a curse," the Ta Kuo said. There was silence from the others.

"He is no curse!" Wong Lin yelled. "He is just a man. That I will show you, I promise. And you will see him die!"

"Then maybe the Golden Dragon is a curse," another Ta Kuo said. "Maybe we should not try to find it any longer."

Wong Lin grew even angrier. "Cowards! Fools! We have come all this way and are very close to being wealthy and having absolute power. Now you want to run."

There was a heavy silence as Wong Lin looked from man to man.

"Those of you who want to follow me, come with me now. Those of you who are cowards I never want to see again."

Three of Wong Lin's men—one of them wounded—turned their horses and started back toward Reno. The others turned to Wong Lin and pledged their loyalty until the end.

"But how do we find the Golden Dragon?" one of them asked Wong Lin. "Lee has escaped us."

"He has not escaped us," Wong Lin said through clenched teeth. "This desert is very dry and there are tracks.'' He pointed into the distance. ''You can see that he is going to the Golden Dragon right now as we speak. He does not want us to find it. But we will. Yes, we will. And Lee and that gunfighter will enter tonight's darkness as dead men.''

The dry, packed ground exploded into dust under the horses' hooves. Lee was desperate to reach the caves and find the Golden Dragon. Though Wong Lin didn't know the secret of the blue stone that marked the chamber, Lee felt that the Ta Kuos would search extensively and could stumble upon the dragon anyway. He believed that his only hope to keep it out of their hands was to get into the caves first and bury the dragon.

While they rode, Lassiter would at times turn to look back and see if the Ta Kuos had gained on them. Lee was looking for the hills that held the caves and the Golden Dragon, and they were riding slower than Wong Lin and his men. Lassiter figured the Ta Kuos would be upon them in the space of just three to four more miles. If they didn't reach the caves right away, there wouldn't be any time to search for and bury the dragon.

Then Lee pointed ahead and shouted. As they rounded a hill, there appeared before them a maze of caves that ran through mixed rock and salt-tainted soils. It seemed like a formation of the land unto itself within the vast stretches of stunted brush and alkali.

Lee was ecstatic, but there were a great number of openings into the hillside and there was no way to tell which one might possibly take them to the Golden Dragon.

Lee scanned the surrounding area until he found a hilltop that caught his eye. It was barren, except for two stunted trees that grew together just below the summit.

''That the hill Tun tell me about,'' Lee stated. ''But

sun not yet in right position. Soon, though. I will go to hill and wait."

Lanna pointed back toward the trail. "You haven't got time to wait," she said. "The Ta Kuos will be here any moment. If they see you up there, they'll kill you. You've got to come into the caves with us for cover."

"Have no choice but to go on hill," Lee said. "Won't find Golden Dragon any other way. It do me no good to come this far and for nothing. I go now. I succeed, or I die."

21

LASSITER LED LANNA and her father into the mouth of one of the caves, where they dismounted and hurried inside. Here they discovered a series of interconnected caverns that led deep into the hills. It was too dark to see much, so Lassiter went back outside to collect some of the creosote bush that covered the area. Its sticky surface would make suitable torches.

No sooner were they positioned inside than the Ta Kuos appeared. Lassiter could see that their main interest was on the caverns and that no one was looking into the hills. For the time being, Lee would be safe.

"I don't know if I can hold them back," Lassiter told Lanna and her father. "But if we don't want them jumping into our laps any second, I've got to do something."

Lassiter waited until the Ta Kuos dismounted and began getting ready to come toward the caves. He was certain that the Ta Kuos knew right where they were, for it wasn't hard to see the tracks they had left in coming up to the cave's entrance. He decided to act before the Ta Kuos started for the caves.

Lassiter rushed out from the cave and fired toward the group. Though he was out of handgun range and knew it, Wong Lin and his men dove for cover.

"That will give us at least a little more time before they come into the caves," Lassiter told Lanna and her father when he returned. "I just hope the sun gets to where Lee can find that dragon."

Lassiter's move to put the Ta Kuos back a ways worked for a time. But as Lassiter had suspected, Wong Lin divided his men and sent them into various caves along the hillside. He remained with two of the Ta Kuos to watch the main entrance.

"What are they waiting out there for?" Harold Mitchell asked. "Why don't they search with the others?"

"Their leader has gained a little wisdom, I believe," Lassiter replied. "He wants to watch this entrance and be sure we don't come out."

"Are we going to just stay here and wait for Lee then?" Lanna asked.

"There's no purpose to it now," Lassiter said. "Now we're better off going through these caves and search for the Golden Dragon ourselves. We'd be in a bad fix if some of the Ta Kuos came through these tunnels behind us and managed to get us trapped here."

Lassiter had no sooner gotten the words out of his mouth than three Ta Kuos appeared behind them. They had come from an adjoining tunnel and were equally as surprised to see Lassiter resting with Lanna and her father.

One of the Ta Kuos got off a shot that zinged off the rocks next to Lassiter. As he rolled to one side, he pulled his Colt and shot the hatchet man twice, sending the other two for cover.

As soon as Lassiter had started the other way down

the tunnel with Lanna and her father, the other two Ta Kuos quickly gave chase. They shot wildly, loosening rocks from the ceiling of the caverns. Lassiter pulled Lanna and her father behind him and held his position against one wall of the tunnel until the two Ta Kuos were nearly upon them.

He judged where the sounds of their footsteps would bring them and came off the wall to face them. The darkness of the tunnel was suddenly lit by flame from the barrels of his Colts, and the two hatchet men fell yelling.

The gunfire brought more of the other Ta Kuos through the tunnels. They were coming from two directions and as their yelling voices grew nearer, Lanna asked Lassiter, "How are we going to keep from being trapped?"

"We're going to have to make a stand somewhere," he said. "There's no other way out that I know of."

Harold Mitchell had his Colt ready. "I can shoot better when I'm not on a bouncing horse."

"Get ready, then," Lassiter told him.

He took them down the tunnel a ways, looking for large rocks that could provide some cover when the Ta Kuos converged on them. He lit some of the brush to see by and Lanna suddenly pulled on his arm.

"Look," she said, pointing to a small hole in the wall near the floor. "That might be a way out."

"It's worth a try," Lassiter said.

Lassiter waited while Lanna and her father crawled through the small hole. Then he extinguished his torch and followed after them. As he came to his feet, he could hear the Ta Kuos rushing past in the tunnel, talking among themselves. Finally, they were gone.

"It's really dark in here," Lanna said then. "I don't see any light coming from anywhere. There's no other way in except that small hole."

Lassiter lit the torch again and held it up. The chamber was not very large. The surfaces of its walls and low ceiling looked uniform and regular. It appeared to have been mostly man-made. And Lanna was right—there was no way out but the way they had come in.

"What's in here?" Harold Mitchell then asked. "I feel strange."

As Lassiter moved toward the back of the chamber, the shadows became filled with light. Lassiter then realized Harold Mitchell was right, there was something in there with them.

Against the farthest back wall was the skeleton of a man, lying in a heap on the cavern floor.

"I don't like this," Lanna said.

Lassiter then moved his torch to another position and quickly stepped back in alarm. A large piece of metal gleamed furiously in the light.

"It's the Golden Dragon!" Lanna said, her breath leaving her.

She crowded next to Lassiter, afraid of the object. Harold Mitchell stood on the other side of Lassiter and stared. The dragon—nearly five feet long and made of pure gold—was resting on a flat rock, assuming a position of carved defiance. It was half-lizard and half-snake, with a formation of spinelike scales along the backbone, tapering from a larger middle to a long tail and a curved neck that supported a horned head and an open mouth filled with long sharp teeth.

The tongue was a length of flame and the eyes were set close together under tight, angry lids—ruby eyes which gleamed like fire in the torchlight. Its body was hunched in a fighting stance, its twisted legs resting on knurled, eagle-taloned feet with sharp, ivory claws.

"That is really something," Lassiter said in awe. "I've never seen anything like it in my life."

"It's a horrible thing," Harold Mitchell said. "I wouldn't want anything to do with that."

"It certainly looks like something that people would

kill over," Lanna observed. "Or maybe something that could kill people itself. Let's get out of here."

"It's not alive," Lassiter pointed out to both of them. "It's not going to come at us."

"It seems like it to me," Lanna said. "I want to go. Now."

"Do you think we can bring Lee back here?" Lassiter asked Harold Mitchell. "Can you help me remember where this is?"

"I don't know," he said, unable to take his eyes off the dragon.

"I don't want to remember where this is," Lanna then said. "I just want away from that thing—forever!"

Lanna suddenly rushed toward the opening through which they had entered the chamber. Without hesitation, she crawled through.

"Wait!" her father yelled after her. "Those tongs could be out there anywhere."

But Lanna was through the opening and running in the dark of the tunnel. Lassiter and Harold Mitchell made their way through and called out to her. They started running toward her and saw suddenly that Lanna had turned and was rushing back toward him. There were a number of Ta Kuos right behind her, and one of them was Wong Lin.

As Lanna rushed to him, Lassiter put out his torch and fired at the Ta Kuos, sending them back a ways to find cover. He realized there was no way out but the way they had come in, and that meant they were trapped.

Wong Lin and his men began shooting. Lassiter held Lanna and her father back against the tunnel wall and stayed low himself to avoid the bullets that rang off the rocks all around them. But even more dangerous were the rocks that began falling from the walls and ceiling. The noise of the gunfire was shaking the rocks loose.

"This place is starting to cave in!" Lanna yelled at Lassiter.

"Let's go," Lassiter told Lanna and her father. "We've got to get out of here."

Lassiter led the way, firing his Colts and moving from one side of the tunnel to another. Lanna and her father followed closely, trying to avoid rocks and bullets.

As Lassiter stopped in the darkness to reload, the Ta Kuos ahead of them continued to shoot blindly, causing more and more rocks and dust to fall. Finally, their was a rumble and the shooting stopped. A section of the tunnel up ahead and collapsed.

Lassiter lit his torch again. The dust was almost totally blinding, but he led Lanna and her father ahead to where they found a section of the tunnel nearly blocked off.

"We're trapped," Harold Mitchell said.

"Don't give up hope just yet," Lassiter told him.

With his torch ablaze Lassiter began searching the rocks for a hole. He found a leg and a hand sticking out of the fallen rocks. Then a shoulder and an arm with a sling attached to it.

"It looks like the Ta Kuos have had it," Lassiter said.

Lassiter moved on, looking for a way out. He held the torch up and saw that near the top of the tunnel, a crack of light appeared.

Lassiter handed the torch to Lanna. "Hold this, and don't burn your hands."

With Lanna holding the creosote torch, Lassiter began digging and pulling rocks down. Finally he had created a hole big enough to crawl through. He took the torch from Lanna and helped her through. After her father had gone through also, he scrambled up toward the light.

They found themselves near the main entrance. There was continual rumbling now throughout the caverns. Outside, they found Lee rushing up to them.

"I saw the stone!" Lee yelled. "I know where Golden Dragon is now."

Lanna stopped him. "You don't want to go in there."

"What?" Lee asked.

"The tunnels are caving in," Lanna said.

"But I have to get to Golden Dragon," Lee said.

"You don't have to worry about the dragon now," Lassiter said. "Wong Lin and his Ta Kuos won't be coming out. And that dragon won't do them any good in their condition."

Lassiter then told him about finding the arm with the sling sticking out of the rocks. Lee was relieved in part, but still wanted to see what he had come all the way from San Francisco to save.

"Believe me, you don't want to risk your life for it," Lanna told him. "It might not be all that you've imagined it to be."

"You saw it?" Lee asked her. He looked to all of them. "You all saw Golden Dragon?"

"We saw it," Lassiter acknowledged. "But whatever that thing is, there's nothing good about it. You're better off not having seen it, believe me."

Lee shrugged. "I take your word for it." He looked to the entrance of the caverns, where more dust was billowing out from yet another cave-in. "I guess nobody ever see Golden Dragon again."

"I guess not," Lassiter said.

"As far as I'm concerned, I never want to see any part of this desert again," Harold Mitchell stated. "And I'm ready to get back to Reno."

Everyone agreed. Lee informed them that he had decided to go across to the edge of the mountains to see Tun once again. If Tun was willing to take him as a student, Lee wanted to remain and learn from him.

Harold Mitchell shook his hand and Lanna hugged him. She blinked a few times, then smiled.

"I wish you the best, Lee," she told him. "Without

you, I wouldn't be worrying about my life now. I don't know if I'd even be around at all. They would have had to kill me before I would have let them shanghai me."

Lee smiled and pointed to Lassiter. "Yes, you and I both not have good future without this man. I guess I forget about shooting guns now. I never get as good as him, and there no use in being second best."

With the sun falling, Lee headed out toward Tun's cave, and Lassiter rode toward Reno with Lanna and her father. The trip back to Reno was a mostly silent one, crossing the desert with a full moon. When they reached Reno, Harold Mitchell booked Lanna and himself on a train almost ready to leave for Utah. They would then catch a stage back up to Glitter Creek.

Lassiter learned the next train due to pass through on its way to San Francisco wasn't until the next day, and he wasn't ready to wait that long. He decided he would ride back over the mountains to San Francisco, where he would pick up his horse and head back into the Rocky Mountains.

"Do you think you'll ever get back up into our neck of the woods?" Lanna asked Lassiter.

"It's hard to tell," Lassiter said. "But I sure know where to come when I want to have dinner with a pretty lady."

"You know where to come if you want to spend your life having dinners with this lady," Lanna told him. "You know that. Just remember it."

He watched Lanna and her father board the train. She waved to him out the window and he nodded and tipped his hat. Lassiter turned his horse toward the Sierras and started his ride back toward San Francisco. In a couple of days he would have his own stallion again. And some trail would take Lassiter to where he could see the stars and feel the wind against his face.